KILLER SECRETS

Katie Reus

Copyright © 2011 by Katie Reus

All rights reserved. Except as permitted under the U.S. Copyright Act of 1976, no part of this publication may be reproduced, distributed, or transmitted in any form or by any means, or stored in a database or retrieval system, without the prior written permission of the author. Thank you for buying an authorized version of this book and complying with copyright laws. You're supporting writers and encouraging creativity.

Cover art: Jaycee of Sweet 'N Spicy Designs
JRT Editing
Author website: http://www.katiereus.com

Publisher's Note: This is a work of fiction. Names, characters, places, and incidents are either the products of the author's imagination or used fictitiously, and any resemblance to actual persons, living or dead, or business establishments, organizations or locales is completely coincidental.

Killer Secrets/Katie Reus. -- 1st ed.

ISBN-13: 978-1500728434
ISBN-10: 1500728438

Praise for the novels of Katie Reus

"Sinful, Sexy, Suspense... Katie Reus pulls you in and never lets go."
—*New York Times* bestselling author, Laura Wright

"Has all the right ingredients: a hot couple, evil villains, and a killer action-filled plot. . . . [The] Moon Shifter series is what I call Grade-A entertainment!" —Joyfully Reviewed

"Reus strikes just the right balance of steamy sexual tension and nail-biting action….This romantic thriller reliably hits every note that fans of the genre will expect." —*Publisher's Weekly*

"Explosive danger and enough sexual tension to set the pages on fire . . . fabulous!" —*New York Times* bestselling author, Alexandra Ivy

"Nonstop action, a solid plot, good pacing and riveting suspense…"
—*RT Book Reviews (4.5 Stars)*

"Wow! This powerful, passionate hero sizzles with sheer deliciousness. I loved every sexy twist of this fun & exhilarating tale. Katie Reus delivers!" —Carolyn Crane, RITA award winning author

Continued…

"You'll fall in love with Katie's heroes." —*New York Times* bestselling author, Kaylea Cross

"A sexy, well-crafted paranormal romance that succeeds with smart characters and creative world building."—Kirkus Reviews

"*Mating Instinct*'s romance is taut and passionate . . . Katie Reus's newest installment in her Moon Shifter series will leave readers breathless!" —Stephanie Tyler, *New York Times* bestselling author

"Reus has definitely hit a home run with this series. . . . This book has mystery, suspense, and a heart-pounding romance that will leave you wanting more." —Nocturne Romance Reads

"Katie Reus pulls the reader into a story line of second chances, betrayal, and the truth about forgotten lives and hidden pasts." —The Reading Café

"If you are looking for a really good, new military romance series, pick up *Targeted*! The new Deadly Ops series stands to be a passionate and action-riddled read." —That's What I'm Talking About

"I could not put this book down. . . . Let me be clear that I am not saying that this was a good book *for* a paranormal genre; it was an excellent romance read, *period*." —All About Romance

CHAPTER ONE

Eve Newman pressed her back up against one of the stone pillars at the entrance to the Underwood's long, winding driveway. She wasn't exactly sure what she was doing here but for the tenth time in the last hour she regretted her decision to put any credence to that anonymous email. *'Want the story of the year? Underwood mansion. Nine o'clock. Tonight. Don't trust anyone and don't be seen.'*

The cryptic message annoyed her. As one of the few journalists in the small town of Hudson Creek, Texas, she'd had no choice but to follow up on the lead. She certainly wasn't going to give the story to someone else and her curiosity wouldn't let her ignore it.

Since she'd grown up here—and had attended a few high school parties at the mansion courtesy of Tara Underwood—she knew exactly where the security cameras were and how to avoid them.

Squashing the twinge of guilt at using that knowledge against her friend's parents, she peered around the pillar. A full moon hung in the sky illuminating only one car. The District Attorney's Mercedes. Made sense Richard Underwood would be home. She doubted he'd sent her the email because what could Richard be doing to warrant such a mysterious message?

Frowning, she glanced down the long street. The up-scale neighborhood was quiet tonight. Still she tucked her long hair into the thick, knitted cap she'd brought and pulled it down low on her head. Without it, her strawberry blonde hair would be like a beacon for any-one to see. Wearing all black and feeling like a thief, she gritted her teeth and sprinted toward the closest oak tree on the property.

Using the darkness and shadows as her friend, she hurried toward the six foot wall surrounding the prop-erty. Her heart pounded wildly and her palms were clammy inside her gloves. She hadn't even told her boss where she was going. But she wasn't totally unprepared. Her Glock 33 was tucked into the back of her pants as a precaution.

As she crept down the length of the brick wall, the sound of a male voice shouting made her pause. She was right in line with the main house but the voice was far-ther away. Almost like it was outside, but too muted. *The pool house.*

Careful to dodge two of the security cameras, she moved fast until she was hunkered down by a couple of overgrown bushes. The lights from the pool house were on, but the blinds were shut. She could see two silhouettes moving around inside. The shapes were too blurry to make out whether the people were male or female.

After glancing around the back of the large property to make sure she hadn't missed any more video cameras, she pulled her cap down lower and began making her way across the grass. It was almost nine o'clock so maybe this meeting was what her anonymous email had been talking about.

A man started shouting again and her curiosity surged higher. She couldn't understand what he was saying but his tone was angry. As she started to move closer, the very distinctive sound of gunshots erupted.

Pop. Pop. Pop. One shot right after another.

Then silence. Adrenaline surged through her like a raging river.

She was standing right in the middle of the yard like a freaking target. Not caring if any of the cameras caught her, she ran toward the cluster of bushes lining the pool house and jumped behind them. She needed to call the cops, but hiding was her number one priority. Eve held her breath and when there were no other sounds she raised her head and tried to look in one of the windows.

The blinds were drawn shut and she could barely see through the sliver between the edge of the blinds and the edge of the window. Immediately she spotted a pair of male dress shoes. Expensive shoes. From the awkward angle it looked like they were attached to someone lying on the ground. Someone not moving.

Slowly, she reached down to grab her cell phone out of her pocket. When she patted nothing, she inwardly cursed. Sure, she'd remembered her gun but she'd left her damn phone in her purse...which was in her car a few blocks over. A lot of good that would do her now.

If someone was dead or dying, she had to get help.

The sound of a door opening then slamming shut made her duck back down into the bushes. She hoped her dark clothing would help conceal her. Even though she hated to move, she withdrew her gun.

Her hand shook slightly but she'd spent countless hours on the range. When the time came, she knew she could use it if she had to. At the sound of footsteps running away, she inched above the foliage only to see the French door that led into the main house slam shut.

A light went on in one of the rooms downstairs then a few seconds later a light upstairs flipped on.

Taking a chance, she hurried from her hiding place and ran to the front of the pool house. Eve cringed as her boots thudded against the stone patio at the front of the small structure but she couldn't do anything about it.

Her time was limited.

Easing the door open with her shoulder, she kept her gun tight in her hands. Her gut roiled at the sight in front of her. Next to the splatters of blood on the slick tile floor, the pale yellow walls seemed garish and too bright. Right beside the billiard table in the corner of the room, Allen *freaking* Martin lay on his back. His dark, unblinking eyes were wide open, and a look of shock covered his handsome face. Her gut told her he was dead.

Eve hadn't exactly liked the guy but, *damn*. She quickly peeked back out the door and when she saw no one was there, hurried over to the body. After spending months embedded with the troops in Afghanistan, she'd seen her share of dead bodies and she had a feeling he was gone, but she checked his pulse anyway.

Nothing.

Crimson slowly seeped out from the three gaping holes in his chest and was beginning to pool on the tile floor. The coppery scent of death filled her nostrils.

Instinctively she started to step back. She didn't want to contaminate the crime scene and she really didn't want to leave any evidence behind. She had no business being here but she did need to call the cops—even if she didn't have much faith in their abilities. Her car was blocks over and she couldn't waste that much time. She hoped Martin had a phone on him.

Avoiding the growing pool of blood, she felt the front of his jacket pocket until she found his cell. Once her fingers clasped around it she hurried back to the door. When she looked out she saw the light upstairs in the main house shut off.

Crap!

Whoever had done this was probably coming back. She just couldn't wrap her mind around the fact that Richard Underwood had shot Allen Martin. Sure, Martin was sleazy, but Underwood was a good, honest DA. Or she'd thought he was. Now it looked like he might be a killer.

Hurrying back the way she'd come, she paused once she was outside the fenced yard to use Martin's phone. She dialed 911.

As soon as the operator picked up she started whispering into the phone. "There's a dead body at the Underwood mansion. 685 Kent Ave."

"Ma'am, can you please repeat that address?"

"There's a dead body in the pool house behind the Underwood mansion on Kent Avenue. Allen Martin has been shot three times in the chest and he's not breathing. Hurry!"

"Ma'am, are you telling me that Allen Martin is dead in the DA's pool house?" Eve doubted the operator was supposed to let her disbelief show, but in a small town the woman would have no doubt where the Underwood mansion was and exactly who owned it.

She sighed at the woman's question. The dispatcher should already be contacting a patrol car. Another strike against the police department of Hudson Creek. They'd screwed up the prosecution of the man who'd killed Eve's parents. Why not screw this up too?

"Yes, that's what I'm telling you. Send someone *now*. The killer is still here." It was hard to keep her voice a whisper when she wanted to shout at the operator.

"We're sending a patrol over but I need to know who I'm speaking to."

Not freaking likely.

Instead of answering, Eve hung up. She couldn't afford to say anything else. She'd trespassed on the property and admitting that to the sheriff would give him an excuse to waste hours interrogating her.

As she glanced around she realized no one must have heard the shots because the street was deathly quiet. She desperately wanted to wait around and make sure the cops showed up but knew she couldn't. If they found her here she'd be in a world of trouble. Hurrying, she continued her escape down the sidewalk.

When the phone she'd taken started ringing, she jumped. The caller ID screen said restricted.

"Hey, I hear it," a thick, accented male voice said from behind the fence of the Underwood's place.

Panic jumped in Eve's chest. She pressed the end button, effectively silencing the call as she started running down the sidewalk. Her boots thudded loudly but there was nothing she could do about it. She wanted to turn the phone off completely but didn't have time to waste.

"Hey! Stop!" the same voice shouted behind her a few moments later.

A sharp pop blasted through the air and the trunk of one of the trees lining the street splintered. The pop sounded again and Eve felt a gush of air rush past her face. Someone was shooting at her!

Taking a sharp right, she darted across the Hawkins' lawn. Even though they had an incredible house their security was shit and she knew they had an opening in their wrought iron fence in the backyard. If she could just make it.

Her leg muscles strained and for the first time in years she was thankful for her daily jogging routine. Pumping her arms and legs, she cleared the edge of the house. A spotlight on the side of the house flipped on— likely motion sensors—but she didn't pause.

It almost felt as if someone was breathing down her neck, but she knew it was fear and adrenaline surging through her. Then she heard a muttered curse farther behind than before. At least they weren't still shooting. Probably because whoever it was didn't want to draw more attention to themselves.

She needed to make it to the opening and hoped no one saw her slip through. Her car was on the next street over. Her heart pounded that erratic tattoo against her chest as she dove over a cluster of bushes lining the back fence.

Blood rushed loudly in her ears as she began to slowly crawl toward the opening. When the phone started ringing again, her chest tightened. They were trying to track her using the sound. She silenced it again then slid the back casing off. She'd only have a few seconds to do this. Sliding the SIM card out, she put it in her pocket then left the phone lying in the dirt.

As she continued crawling, she pulled her gun out. When she reached the small gap in the fence she shimmied under it. Ignoring the dirt coating her hands and the underbrush caught in her cap and clothes, she shoved up and ran through the neighboring backyard.

After risking a brief glance behind her, she saw she wasn't being followed. She allowed herself a small measure of relief but didn't stop running. Even if they were still looking for her, they weren't going to find her. She wouldn't let them.

Unfortunately she couldn't go home. She hadn't recognized the accented voice, but she couldn't be sure whoever had been chasing her hadn't identified her. That left one place to go.

Macklin wasn't going to be happy to see her, but Mr. Tall, dark, and too-sexy-for-his-own-good would have to deal with it. He was one of the few people on the planet she would trust with her life.

CHAPTER TWO

Mac paused as he ran a towel over his damp hair. Then he heard the sound again. Someone was banging on his front door. Insistently. He glanced at the watch he'd left on his bathroom counter. It was almost ten. Normally he'd be in bed by now and so would most of his men, but they'd had trouble with some of the cattle getting out after a section of one of his fences had been intentionally knocked down. By drug smugglers no doubt. They were getting worse in this area and he was fed up with it.

Without bothering to put on clothes, he headed toward the front door. That's when he heard the one voice that had the ability to make him go rock hard in seconds.

"Macklin Quinn, I know you're in there! You better open this door right now!" Eve's shouts were followed by three more bangs.

For such a petite woman she had a loud knock. Shaking his head, he jerked the door open.

"Damn it, Mac..." She trailed off as she stared at him. Unabashedly her eyes tracked down his bare chest to the damp towel hanging on his hips.

Her peaches and cream complexion often gave away her emotions and now was no different. Those dark eyes of hers flared with momentary interest as they reached the top of his towel. When her gaze landed on his growing erection, her cheeks tinged an adorable pink and she quickly looked up. "Uh...do you have company?"

"No." The only company he wanted was her. In his bed. But that wasn't going to happen. So why was she here?

She sighed and visibly relaxed. "I need a place to stay tonight."

Mac wouldn't mind accommodating her but he knew her well enough that she wasn't looking to jump into his bed. If only. He frowned as he took in her appearance. "What the hell happened to you, Eve?" The question came out harsher than he intended. Her hair was hidden by a dark cap and she wore all black, like some sort of cat burglar. Dirt smudges covered her face and...were those leaves sticking out of her collar?

She bit her bottom lip and eyed him nervously. "Aren't you going to let me in?"

Sighing because he couldn't say no to her, he stepped back. When he shut the door behind her, she wrung her hands in front of her stomach. "I did something stupid tonight but I'm not going to tell you what it is if you're going to give me a lecture."

Oh, shit. If the stubborn woman was actually admitting she'd done something stupid, he'd no doubt need a shot of whiskey. Stepping further into the foyer, he motioned with his hand. "Come on. Let's go to my office."

Once they reached his office she tugged the cap off her head and all those gorgeous strawberry blonde waves fell around her face and shoulders. He resisted the very real urge to reach over and run his hands through her hair. To cup her head tight, pull her close, and—

"Can't you put on a shirt or something," she muttered as she sat on the cushy chair across from his desk.

He stiffened at her words. Instinctively he rubbed a hand over his left side and all the hideous, scarred skin. It didn't hurt anymore and most days he forgot about it but now...he wished he *had* put on a shirt. He didn't like her seeing this deformed side of him.

Before he could respond she continued. "Don't get that hurt look on your face. You *know* I didn't mean it because of your scars."

"Then why'd you say it?"

Her cheeks flushed again as she found a spot on the wall behind him to stare at. "Because I can't think with you half-naked." The way she spoke through gritted teeth told him she meant it even if she didn't want to admit it.

It shouldn't please him, but it did. Probably too much. He bit back a grin because it would only annoy her. Eve was one of the few women he knew who didn't focus on superficial stuff. And she'd been one of the few people who hadn't acted like she felt sorry for him when he'd moved home injured, scarred and pissed off at the world. No, she'd told him to get over himself and be thankful he was alive. "Stay put and don't get into trouble for sixty seconds, okay?" Without waiting for a response he hurried to his room and tossed on a pair of faded jeans and a sweater. He found her sitting in the same spot with that worried expression on her face. "What's going on?"

"I just saw a murder," she blurted. As she launched into a crazy story he was torn between shaking her and hugging her. When she finally finished she tucked a wayward curl behind her ear and stared at him with wide eyes.

"You really think Richard Underwood killed Martin?" Underwood was the squeaky clean DA of Hudson Creek whereas Allen Martin was one of the sleaziest men Mac knew. Martin owned five car dealerships around the immediate area and lived up to that greasy car salesman cliché. But that didn't mean he deserved to be shot.

"I...I don't know who killed him, but Richard's car was outside the house. Whoever chased after me wasn't him. That much I'm pretty sure of. The guy had an accent."

"How do you know?"

"When he called the phone—"

"That you *took*." It was smart she'd taken it to call the police, but stupid that she'd been there by herself in the first place.

She gritted her teeth. "Don't interrupt. When he called Martin's phone he said 'I hear it' or something like that."

"Then he was probably talking to someone."

"Yeah." Her eyes glazed over for a moment and he could practically see the wheels turning in her head.

"What is it?"

Instantly she jerked out of her trance and cleared her throat. "Nothing. Can I stay here tonight? I don't think whoever it was recognized me but just in case I'd feel safer here."

"You need to call Sheriff Marcel," he said mildly, knowing it wouldn't make a bit of difference in convincing her.

She shook her head. "No way. Those jerks don't know what they're doing. They'll probably think it was me or something."

Mac bit back a sigh because he understood her anger. Her parents had been killed by a drunk driver and the current sheriff's predecessor had botched the entire process. It had gone to trial but when they'd lost the blood test results with the other driver's blood alcohol content, it had been over before it began. And it didn't help that the attending officer had been a new recruit and had gotten so flustered on the stand, the defendant's attorney had ripped him apart.

"You can't lump Marcel and his guys in with...his predecessor." Mac didn't even like to say Frank Reed's name. It only made pain flash in Eve's eyes and seeing that was like someone stabbing him.

"I can do whatever I want," she said, though she'd lost most of her steam. "Besides, Marcel's mad at me because he thinks I got in the way of his last investigation. I don't want to give him more ammunition against me."

"He's pissed at you because you keep turning him down for dates." How did she not know that?

Eve blinked twice then frowned at him. "He's not *serious*."

Mac snorted. Oh yes, the sheriff was. He'd been after Eve since she'd moved back to town a couple years ago. And he wasn't the only one. It shouldn't bother Mac. He had no claim on her. But damn if he didn't want her for himself. Things between them would be too complicated though and he couldn't travel down that road with her. "Fine, I'll place a call to him tomorrow and—"

She jumped out of her seat. "No! I already have a plan and I don't need your help. Tomorrow I'm going to head to the station and act like I'm following up on a lead about Allen Martin. I can't accuse the DA of anything until I'm positive he's involved in this."

"You don't think showing up at the station is suspicious?"

Her lips pulled into a thin line as she shook her head. "I'm a journalist. I'm always bugging the sheriff about stuff."

Mac scrubbed a hand over his face. It took all his self-control not to call the sheriff but in his gut he knew it wouldn't do much good. She'd already called the cops and if he told the sheriff what he knew, Eve could get in a lot of trouble. Not to mention it would break her trust. Not something he could do and live with himself. Standing, he pushed his chair back. "I'm beat so..."

"Sorry, I know I barged in on you. If you have a T-shirt or something I could borrow to sleep in I promise I'll stay out of your hair."

His lower abdomen burned with need at the thought of her wearing something of his. Instead of responding—because he didn't trust his voice—he grunted something incomprehensible and motioned for her to follow him.

Hating how tight his skin felt and the uncomfortable sensation coursing through him, he stalked down the hall to his room. The five bedroom house was big for just him and now he felt as if it were taking forever to make it across the house.

As he finally entered his room he cringed. A pile of unclean clothes lay in one corner and he'd tossed his dirty work clothes at the end of his unmade bed. Nice.

Behind him, Eve chuckled under her breath and muttered something about him being 'such a guy' but he ignored it. He was definitely feeling like a guy right now. Being near her was making his brain short-circuit and giving him a raging hard-on. It was embarrassing that he couldn't control himself.

He shifted uncomfortably as he jerked open one of his dresser drawers and rummaged around until he found one of his old Marine Corps T-shirts. It was about a decade old and he'd gotten it when he'd first enlisted. Since that first year in he'd put on a lot of muscle so while it would still be big, it wouldn't completely swallow her. Next he grabbed a pair of sweatpants that would definitely be too big but it was all he had.

When he handed the bundle of clothes to her, their fingers brushed and they both froze. An undeniable electric arc of energy sparked between them and made him almost jerk back.

Staring into her dark eyes, he fought that familiar drowning sensation he experienced every single time she was near. She made him feel like a randy teenager. Out of control and horny all the time. He could lose himself with her. His brain struggled to think of something—anything—to say but she beat him to the punch.

It vaguely registered that this was exactly why he avoided her.

She mumbled 'thanks' as she took the clothes but she still didn't make a move to leave. Just stared at him as if she wanted him to kiss her. Ten years ago it wouldn't have surprised him, but it did now. She wasn't a teenager anymore. She was a beautiful, grown woman and shouldn't want anything to do with a roughneck like him.

But damn, did he ever want to follow through with this kiss.

More than just a kiss. He wanted to taste her, dominate her, make her forget anyone but he existed... The flare of lust in her eyes was too much.

Reaching out, he cupped her cheek. When he did, she sucked in a shaky breath but didn't pull away.

He wanted to tell her to go but the words wouldn't form. And her skin was so soft and *female*. He rubbed the pad of his callused thumb over her cheek. Her eyes grew heavy-lidded for a moment.

He could practically feel the heat rolling off her. Stepping forward slowly, he gave her time to back away as he closed the distance between them. But she didn't.

She met him halfway. Before he could react, her hands slid up his chest and around his neck.

He was so screwed. The thought rang in his head crystal clear. Once he kissed Eve he knew there'd be no going back for him.

As he leaned down, her mouth parted invitingly. When their lips touched he felt the reaction straight to his center. Her tongue stroked against his, playfully at first. But he didn't want playful.

Something primal burned inside him. He wanted to invade her senses. Make her feel the way he did every time he got close to her. He started to thread his fingers through her thick hair when she froze.

With wide eyes, she pulled back and out of his embrace. She swallowed hard and shook her head. "I can't...we can't...goodnight, Mac." Before he could think of a response, she turned on her heel and hurried out of his room.

After she'd gone he realized he hadn't shown her to a guestroom, but he knew she'd figure it out and pick one. If she didn't, he hoped she'd crawl into bed with him. He scrubbed a hand over his face at the thought. That was definitely wishful thinking.

The only thing he knew was that she wasn't going to the sheriff's by herself tomorrow. The woman could fight him all she wanted but after what she'd told him, he wasn't letting her out of his sight.

Eve, more than anyone, had the ability to drive him insane. He'd known her practically his entire life and he'd been half in love with her for most of it. Things would never work out though. Too many complications and baggage. She was too good for him. Way too good. Part of him was glad she'd realized it before they'd done something stupid tonight. He sure as hell hadn't had the common sense to pull back.

E ve pulled her damp hair back into a ponytail as she
stared at her closet. It was weird to have Mac waiting in her living room while she was getting dressed,
especially after that kiss last night. She'd been ready to
jump in bed with him right then and there. But that
would have been insane. Taking things further would
completely ruin their friendship. A man like him didn't
settle down and it would be foolish to think otherwise.

She didn't understand why the stubborn man had insisted on following her home. And then he'd decided to
wait while she showered and got dressed. After getting a
solid night's sleep she felt better about the fact that no
one had seen her. She'd kept her face hidden and she'd
worn gloves. By now the police probably had someone
in custody and since she'd already copied Allen Martin's
SIM card, she was going to give it to the sheriff anonymously. She felt a little bad about that but chances were,
if she'd left it, it would be destroyed by now. Someone
had wanted it for a reason so that had to be important.

She finally settled on a pair of dark jeans, a plain
black shirt and a black fitted jacket to go over it. She had
a few stops planned today and if she dressed up too

much, people always seemed to be uncomfortable. Maybe it was a Texas thing, she wasn't sure. After grabbing a pair of flat boots and her purse, she found Mac in her living room.

He was staring at a twelve-year-old picture of her and her brother. It had been taken on Mac's ranch, back when his father had run the place. She'd been sixteen at the time and just growing into her body. And she'd developed a massive crush on Mac that summer. He'd noticed her body and her crush.

As she sat on the couch and slid on one of her boots, he turned those ice blue eyes on her and her heart stuttered. "Sure you don't want to fix breakfast or anything before we leave?" he asked.

She shook her head and zipped up the first one. And she didn't want to talk about mundane stuff either. "You remember that summer?" She nodded toward the picture.

He shrugged stiffly but at least he didn't avert his gaze. Yeah, he remembered all right. She could see it on his face.

"You almost kissed me that summer. Would have been my first kiss too." Instead she'd gotten her first one from Billy Johnson later that year. He'd been all tongue and slobber. Not the best experience. Even thinking about it now grossed her out.

"I almost lost my head that summer," he muttered as he shoved his hands into his jeans pockets.

She remembered that day well. Barely eighteen, Mac had been horrified he'd almost made a move on his best friend's little sister. He'd told her he was sorry for what he'd done. She hadn't wanted his apology, she'd wanted him. But after that they'd never talked about it and that summer he and Daniel had enlisted in the Marine Corps together. She hadn't seen Mac much after that but when she had, nothing had ever happened between them—or *almost* happened—again.

Not that she wouldn't have liked it. He'd filled out in all the right places after joining the military. He'd been good looking before but he'd come back ripped and toned and not in that gross gym rat way. Even today he wore his dark hair cropped close. And those blue eyes of his still had the ability to make her melt. Sometimes it felt like he could see right through her, all the way to her fantasies. She wasn't sure why she'd even brought up the almost-kiss when she should be doing everything in her power to avoid talking about anything that involved their lips meshing.

When he didn't say anything else, she plucked her purse off the coffee table and stood. "I appreciate everything you've done for me but you don't need to follow me into town today."

"I'm not following you. You're riding with me. I know you're busy so you can take my truck and do whatever it is you need to do." He spoke as if she had no choice in the matter.

"That's stupid. Besides, what are you going to do for a vehicle?"

"After we go to the sheriff's station you can drop me off at the feed store where I'll catch a ride with Griffin. I've already talked to him." He'd lost a lot of his drawl after being gone for almost a decade, but it came back in full force when he was being extra bossy.

"Mac, that makes no sense—"

"For all we know, Martin's killer is still on the loose. I'm not taking the chance someone recognized you...or saw your car leaving the scene. They could have gotten your license plate number. It's not that hard to track someone that way. I don't want you driving around in your car today. Not until we have more information." By the firm set of his jaw she knew it would be pointless to argue, but sometimes the man riled her up.

"Look, I know I came to you for help last night, but—"

"It's not up for discussion, *darlin'*."

At the word darlin', the argument died on her lips. Didn't he know how to take all the wind out of her sails? "Fine." She might not like his domineering attitude, but a part of her she didn't want to admit existed, kind of liked the way he was insisting on taking care of her.

Over the years they'd butted heads a few times but the way he was acting now was somehow different. Grunting something incomprehensible, he palmed his keys and strode for the front door.

As he trailed in front of her she couldn't help but watch that tight, firm butt. She'd fantasized way too many times what it would be like to grab onto him. Just once. Okay, maybe more than once. Spending more time with him was going to make those cravings worse. Especially now that she'd had a taste of him.

* * *

Eve lived in a ranch-style house in a small subdivision right on the outskirts of town so it took less than ten minutes to reach downtown.

Mac hated everything about what they were doing, but he didn't see another option. At least she hadn't balked too much at driving his truck around today. He might not be able to keep an eye on her all the time but until they figured out who was responsible for Martin's death, it would have to do.

As Eve sat inside Sheriff Marcel's office not-so-subtly drilling the man with questions, Mac took his time pouring a cup of coffee at the table directly outside the office. From what he could tell, the sheriff had an open door policy and kept the coffee stand next to his office for a reason. He wanted to keep a pulse on his officers, something Mac appreciated.

"You can tell whoever your source is that they're mistaken. We followed up on a bogus lead last night to the Underwood's and found nothing there," the sheriff said.

Mac frowned as he stirred sugar he didn't want into the coffee. Anything to drag out his excuse for loitering.

"My source is impeccable," Eve snapped back.

"Not this time, they're not. The pool house was clean. No blood and certainly no body. I wasted good manpower checking out that bogus call."

"No blood?" Eve sounded incredulous. She'd told him that it had been all over the tile floor.

But Mac knew a fast clean up job would have been easy if the cops hadn't been looking too hard. If they'd already gotten it in their minds that it was a prank call then they wouldn't have brought in anyone to check forensics. By now any blood evidence would be wiped clean. Unless of course they decided to go back and check for traces with luminol.

"That's right. The only thing we discovered is that Richard Underwood's car has been stolen. Maybe you can write a story about that." His voice held an edge of sarcasm.

"Stolen?" Eve asked, disbelievingly. "And what about Allen Martin? Anyone see fit to check up on him?"

The sheriff sighed loudly and Mac knew he was reaching the end of his rope. "I did receive a call last night about a prowler roaming around the exclusive Ranch Rock subdivision. A couple houses down from the Underwood's place. Maybe I should be asking where you were last night."

And that was Mac's cue. Grabbing the second Styrofoam cup he'd poured, he casually strode into the office. "Hey, Rob."

Tearing his gaze away from Eve, the sheriff slightly faltered. "Uh, hey Mac. Haven't seen you around in a while. Everything all right?"

Mac nodded as he handed a second cup to Eve. For effect he winked at her and held back a grin as she blushed. "Everything's fine," he said to the sheriff. "I'm waiting on Eve to take me down to the feed store."

"Ah...oh." His frown deepened.

"She had some car trouble this morning so we decided to ride into town together." The way he said 'we' made it obvious that something was going on with them. He wasn't sure she'd out and out lie to the sheriff about last night, but Mac didn't want her saying something that could come back to bite her in the ass later. He would rather divert the subject regarding her whereabouts last night than have her lie.

Next to him Eve choked on her coffee but didn't argue. She grabbed her purse from the floor and stood. "Sorry to have bothered you."

The sheriff stood, eyeing them suspiciously. "Eve, is there something you need to tell me?"

She snorted softly as if that was the last thing she'd ever do then took another sip of her coffee. "Thanks for your time, Sheriff."

Putting his arm around her shoulders, Mac steered her out of the station.

Once they stepped out into the bright sun, she elbowed him. "What was that? Now he thinks you stayed over at my place."

"So?"

She gritted her teeth and tossed the cup of crappy coffee into the trashcan outside the building. "Now everyone is going to think we're together."

And would that be such a bad thing? He followed suit with his cup. The stuff was swill. "It's better than him questioning you about your whereabouts last night."

Immediately she switched gears as they strode across the parking lot toward his truck. "What was that bull about the DA's car being stolen? I *know* what I saw last night. I certainly didn't conjure up a dead body. Or someone chasing me. Or *shooting* at me. I guarantee the patrol cop only glanced at the pool house—if he even did that at all."

Mac didn't respond as he slid into his seat. Eve might be a lot of things but she wasn't crazy and she wasn't a liar. If she said she'd seen Martin's body, she'd seen it. With the less than stellar record of the Hudson Creek P.D., he didn't blame her for not having faith in them.

"I left one tiny detail out about last night," Eve said as he steered out of the lot.

His stomach dropped at her words. "What?"

"I took Martin's SIM card out of his phone before I escaped."

He swore under his breath. It was actually a pretty smart thing to do. "What are you going to do with it?"

"I already copied the numbers this morning. I was going to anonymously mail the card to the police station but now I wonder…"

"It's evidence. You *need* to turn it over." It wasn't necessarily hard to make a body disappear in west Texas so if someone had taken Martin out to the desert to bury him, Mac doubted they'd ever discover his corpse. But if Eve could get the cops riled up enough to dig into things, maybe it wouldn't be a bad thing. He glanced at her as they pulled up to a stoplight.

"I'll do it today." She chewed on her bottom lip as she stared out the windshield.

"What *else* are you thinking of doing?"

"Nothing. I'm simply wondering if there's a way for us to get his phone records."

Mac shook his head and made a right turn when the light switched to green. "Not without a warrant, you know that."

She was silent as he steered into the feed store parking lot. Something that worried him. When she shifted in her seat to face him, he couldn't help himself.

Reaching out, he cupped her cheek. Apparently he really was a masochist. No good could come of this, but feeling her soft skin against his callus, roughened palm was like holding silk. Her mouth parted slightly, invitingly. If he kissed those pink lips now he'd never want to stop. Instead he kissed her forehead lightly and drew back. "Please don't do anything stupid today, Eve."

"I won't." Her voice was raspy and sexy.

"I'll have one of the guys drop me off at your place later tonight. Call me and let me know when you'll be heading home. I'll try to get there at the same time."

For a moment she looked like she might argue but she nodded. "Okay."

Getting out of his truck and leaving her was the last thing he wanted to do but he ordered his body to obey.

CHAPTER FOUR

E ve stupidly lifted her fingers to her forehead after she pulled out of the parking lot. She didn't understand Mac. Since he'd moved back to town he'd kept his distance from her. Not physically, but she could almost feel him withdrawing from her sometimes when they saw each other. And now he wanted to be all sweet and concerned. Not to mention he'd freaking kissed her last night.

She so didn't need that right now. Allen Martin was dead and no one knew about it. Since she obviously couldn't count on the police to do their job, she needed to find out what was going on and find the killer. The DA's car had 'suddenly' been stolen. More likely it had been used to transport a body then disposed of.

She had to get Martin's phone records. If she could find out who he'd been in contact with lately, she might get a lead. A small part of her wanted to tell the sheriff, but she wasn't sure he'd believe her. And if she opened up that can of worms and he didn't, the whole town would know about it by sunset and the killer would have no doubt she'd been the one at the Underwood mansion last night. She'd become a walking target, she *still*

wouldn't have a clue who had killed Martin and the police wouldn't be concerned if they didn't think Martin
was dead.

Her money was on the DA, but what if it was his
wife? Or someone who worked for them? And who was
the guy with the accent who'd chased her?

Shaking her head, she put her hands-free earpiece in
and called her boss. After letting him know she planned
to run down a few interviews, she was almost to her
destination. When she steered into Iris Bunwell Martin's driveway she braced herself. Iris, or Bunny, as she
liked to call herself, was nice enough. Sometimes she
was a lot to take in though. Big blonde hair, big voice,
big...other assets.

Bunny opened the door a few seconds after Eve rang
the doorbell. Her blue eyes widened a fraction, then surprising concern filled her expression. "Hi, Eve. Is everything all right?"

Eve cleared her throat, hating that she had to question Bunny. They weren't friends but they were ac-
quaintances. Bunny and her mother had been on a few
charitable boards together. That was the one bad thing
about living in a smaller town. She didn't literally know
everyone but some days it felt like it. "I wondered if you
had a few minutes to talk about Allen."

Instantly Bunny's features hardened. "Why would I
want to talk about that snake?"

And that's when Eve noticed Bunny wasn't wearing her wedding ring. Interesting. "I was curious if you'd talked to him lately."

Her eyes narrowed. "Tell me you're not sleeping with him too."

"Ew...Uh, sorry, I mean *no*. I'm following up on a lead for a story and wondered when you'd seen him last." Her stomach ached knowing Allen was dead and she had to question Bunny, but she wasn't sure what else to do.

Bunny relaxed and stepped back. "If you're not sleeping with him would you like a cup of tea?"

Nodding, she followed Bunny inside past a sweeping staircase, through a tiled foyer, and into a formal-looking room with all white furniture. When Bunny motioned for her to sit, Eve took a seat on one of the high-backed, uncomfortable-looking chairs and crossed her legs. Discretely she wiped her palms on her pants. She wanted to run for the front door and never look back. Talking to Bunny like this was not only awkward but her insides were all twisted up. Before she could think of something to say, a woman in black pants and a starched white shirt appeared with a tray of tea and an assortment of pastries.

Eve didn't want to make small talk but she'd have to if she wanted her answers. She also knew she'd get more cooperation if she was semi-honest. "Bunny, I'm here about a story dealing with Allen. This isn't a social call so I want to make sure that's clear so you don't get the wrong impression."

The other woman smiled wryly. "Sweetheart, I'm not stupid. I haven't seen you since your parent's...ah, well, whatever you're here for, feel free to ask. I might not answer but you can ask anything you want."

That was her go ahead, even if she did feel like crap asking Bunny these questions. As Eve took one of the cups she decided to start with a bolder question. "So you and Allen aren't getting along?"

Bunny snorted in an out of character manner. "That's an understatement. I got tired of him screwing his female staff and God knows who else behind my back."

Well that was certainly motive for murder. Though why she'd commit it at the DA's house was a little weird. "So you haven't seen him lately?"

She shook her head. "I saw him about a week ago before I had the locks changed. He packed a few bags but I have no idea where he is. Probably with one of his tramps. I can't believe I stayed with the bastard so long. Thank God my daddy insisted he sign a pre-nup," she muttered.

Allen might have made a lot of money in the past decade but Bunny came from old money. Even if that left a financial reason out as a motive—and Eve couldn't completely rule it out—revenge was always a classic.

"What kind of story are you working on exactly?" Bunny asked as Eve took a sip of her tea.

"I can't say yet. It's sensitive, but...I wondered if you knew who he'd been in contact with lately?"

Her blonde eyebrows rose. "You mean who has he been sleeping around with?"

Eve shook her head even though she was *very* interested in that. If there was more than one woman, talk about motive. "No. I'm referring to business associates." She cleared her throat and decided to plunge ahead. She couldn't lose by asking. "If you have any of his old phone records or anything that would be great. I'm trying to put together some puzzle pieces for a story."

Bunny eyed her curiously for a second. "Are you going to screw him over?"

Eve sat back at the question. "I don't intend to." She wanted to find out who his killer was. Even if he was a snake, he didn't deserve to be murdered and forgotten about.

The blonde half-smiled and stood. "Well if you can, I'd appreciate it. I can give you a copy of the last few months of his phone records but that's all I've got."

Surprise must have shown on Eve's face because Bunny's toothpaste commercial smile widened. "I don't know why you want the records but if you can stick it to the lying bastard, you have my blessing."

Before Eve could respond, she disappeared from the room. A few minutes later she returned with a stack of papers. "These are all copies and they date back about three months. Whatever you plan to do with them, good luck."

After slipping the papers into her purse and thanking Bunny, Eve made a hasty exit. The second she got to her office she was going to pore over these records. She wasn't sure what she was going to find but if she could figure out who he'd been in contact with recently she might have her first big lead.

As Eve pulled out of the quiet, upscale neighborhood she spotted a black SUV behind her. She thought she might have seen one on her way here but she couldn't be sure. She'd been too focused on that stupid kiss Mac had left on her forehead. She still tingled all over thinking about it and it wasn't even a real kiss. Not like what they'd shared last night.

Steering on to the two lane road that led back to town, she shook those thoughts away. She didn't have time for that right now. When a bright flash caught her attention in the rearview mirror, she frowned.

Why had that jerk turned on his brights? It was daylight. They flashed a couple times so she slowed down. She was already going five miles over the speed limit but if he wanted to pass her, she'd let him. The cops around here didn't give speeders a break so either he was passing through and didn't know any better or he was stupid.

The moment she slowed down the other vehicle rammed into her. She gasped as her head and body jerked forward but she managed to hold onto the wheel.

A surge of adrenaline roared through her when the SUV rammed into her again. She jolted forward again. The sound of metal crunching was unmistakable, but Mac's truck was tougher than her little car would ever dream of being. The big truck took the impact of the hit without crumpling. Her throat seized as her grip on the wheel tightened. Someone coming after her in the middle of the day was insane!

She floored the accelerator and risked a glance in the mirror again. The windows were too tinted to see inside. Even the windshield had a dark strip across the front.

Her heart pounded wildly. With shaking hands she grabbed her purse from the passenger seat. As she tried to dig her phone out, the SUV clipped her again. The truck fishtailed wildly.

Eve struggled to keep a grip on the wheel as her purse slid across the bench seat and slammed into the passenger door.

Sweat bloomed on her forehead. Whoever was doing this was serious and she was out by herself with no way to defend herself.

If this guy managed to run her off the road... No! All she had to do was hold on another couple minutes and she'd be closer to town. And other cars and people.

She watched the rearview mirror as he slowed down then zoomed up again. Taking her eyes off him, she floored the truck again. Hating the high speed and the out of control sensation swelling through her, she held on tight and kept her foot on the gas.

The needle point on the speedometer steadily rose— higher than her car could. When she spotted another car coming toward them on the opposite side of the road, she felt a tiny spike of relief.

She was almost to a local gas station that was always busy. All she had to do was get away from this guy. Whoever it was couldn't be stupid enough to attack her in public.

Easing her foot off the gas, she held her breath and glanced in the rearview mirror. The other driver was doing the same. Looked like he didn't want an audience after all. Now she had a dozen other questions. Maybe someone had seen her last night after all. This attack couldn't be random. Not in a small town like Hudson Creek. Her last story had been about the struggling real estate market. Not exactly motive for murder.

Taking a chance, she ducked down and swooped up her fallen phone from the floorboard. The other car flew past and she knew her window of opportunity was closing. Scrolling to Mac's number—after this she was *so* putting him on speed dial—she pressed send. Calling the cops in a situation like this was laughable. If she knew Mac, he'd be able to help her a heck of a lot faster than anyone else.

The second she hit send, she felt another shock from behind. This one was stronger, harder, and she lost her grip on the phone. And on the wheel.

Crying out, she fought for control but it was no use. The truck tilted on its side as she flew off the side of the road.

Trees flew at her. Blood rushed in her ears so loud it was all she could do not to scream. She tried the brakes but it was useless. The tires weren't even on asphalt.

As the truck hurtled forward she heard the sickening crunch of metal a split-second before she felt the harsh impact throughout her entire body.

Her head slammed into the exploding airbag. She instantly jerked back against the headrest. Her neck ached something awful.

Then silence.

She blinked a few times as something dripped down across her right eye. Blood? She reached up and gingerly touched her forehead. The slight contact made her wince in pain.

Blinking again, she looked around. The truck was still on its side. When it had tipped, her purse and phone had slammed back to the driver's side. The vehicle must have slid sideways because she couldn't see the main road anymore. Just a tree and underbrush.

Clutching onto the strap as if it were her lifeline, she held her purse because it gave her a weird sense of comfort. When she heard male voices nearby, her heart pounded harder and she snapped out of the haziness threatening to overwhelm her.

Escape!

She needed to get out of this death trap. She scrambled to get the seatbelt off. When it finally snapped free she fell sideways onto the driver's window and door. No way out here. The door was pinned against the ground.

Her arms and legs ached as she pushed up and tried to crawl toward the other door, but at least her bones weren't broken.

"I hear movement. Hurry!" a male voice shouted.

It registered that there must be two of them. Maybe the same two who'd killed Allen Martin.

They were close now. Eve stopped trying to climb higher and crouched back down. Even if she managed to get out there was no escape.

They were going to kill her!

CHAPTER FIVE

E ve shrank back against the door. Fear blossomed in her chest with a painful awareness that she was probably going to die. Her heart pounded loudly and blood rushed in her ears. She had no clue who was after her. There would be no witnesses either. A burst of anger surged through her, overwhelming her fear. She wouldn't die without a fight.

Looking around the cabin of the truck, she frantically searched for a weapon. Anything to defend herself. Though if they had guns it wouldn't matter much.

Before she could move, a middle-aged man wearing a Stetson appeared at the top of the broken passenger window. He actually looked concerned. "Ma'am? Are you okay? We saw what that SUV did."

She blinked at him, trying to comprehend what he was saying. *Wait, what? He was here to help her?*

"Ma'am, can you hear me?" His voice was louder this time.

Eve nodded. "Yeah. I think I'm okay." She could at least move.

"Hold on." He shouted orders to someone else that she couldn't see. Then another man appeared next to the front of the truck by the windshield. He had a big stick in his hand.

Fear jumped inside her again and she tried to move back. *What was going on?*

Sirens sounded in the distance but if these two planned to kill her it wouldn't matter. She doubted anyone would make it in time to save her.

Her vision hazed for a moment and she realized more blood was dripping down her face. She tried to wipe it away but her hands shook along with the rest of her.

"Try not to move. We're going to pull the windshield off and get you out!" the second man shouted.

That's why he had the stick. She allowed a kernel of relief to blossom inside her. Staying put—not that she had anywhere to go—she watched as he slid it into the small opening where the windshield had broken away from the frame. Using it as a lever, he pushed it down and the whole windshield started to peel up, frame and all.

The other man grabbed the frame. "I'll hold this, you get her out."

Understanding what they were trying to do, Eve hooked her purse across her middle and held her arms out. As she struggled over the steering wheel, the man dropped the stick and looped his hands under her armpits. Reaching up, she wrapped her arms around his neck and let him pull her out.

Once she was free, he bent and picked her up under her knees. "What are you doing?" she mumbled.

"We've got to get you away from this truck. I doubt it'll explode but we're gonna get you closer to the main road. The cops are on their way."

"Cops?" She didn't remember calling them.

"Yes, ma'am. Don't you worry, help is on the way. We couldn't get the full license plate number for that SUV but we got part of it." The man continued talking as he carried her across the dried grass and spots of bare dirt.

Unbidden tears started streaming down her face the farther he walked. It finally started to register what could have happened if it hadn't been for these two men. "Thank you so much for helping me," she said on a choked sob.

"Ah crap, please don't cry, ma'am. You're going to be fine. I don't think you have any broken bones at least." He stopped near what she assumed was his four-door truck on the side of the road and gently sat her on the crunchy, dried grass. Then he also sat and turned to face her. "Can you understand what I'm saying?"

She glanced at his friend who stood next to them looking just as concerned, then looked back at him. "Yes. The cops are on their way and you don't think I'm hurt."

"Good." He nodded then pulled out a plaid handkerchief. Putting it against the top of her forehead, he asked. "Can you hold this in place?"

Nodding, she replaced his hand with her own and held it. Awareness of the stinging sensation skittered across her face at the contact but it was bearable. She was alive. At this point she figured anything was bearable.

* * *

"Can't you go any faster?" Mac asked Griffin through gritted teeth.

"I can't pass the ambulance." Griffin was so calm, Mac wanted to slug him. He'd gotten a call from Eve then heard what sounded like a horrific accident. From the sound of things, some men had apparently helped her out of the truck but he didn't know if she was okay.

His foot tapped against the floorboard impatiently as they flew down the road. He'd called in a favor from a friend at the sheriff's station and found out that a single car accident had been reported around the same time he'd gotten the call from Eve.

As the ambulance slowed down, all his muscles tensed. When he saw his mangled truck turned on its side off from the main two-lane road his heart jumped wildly. *Eve had been driving that.*

Before Griffin had fully stopped Mac jumped out and ran past the two paramedics pulling a stretcher out. He heard another siren in the distance—likely a police car—but he ignored it and sprinted toward another truck sitting on the side of the road. When he cleared the front of it, he almost tripped.

Eve sat next to the truck on the small incline with two ranchers he recognized. "Eve." All he could manage was her name.

Holding a handkerchief to her head, she looked up at him. When her eyes started to water, he lost a decade of his life. The only time he'd seen her cry had been at her parents' funeral.

He ignored the other two men as he knelt in front of her. Taking him completely by surprise, she lunged at him and threw her arms around his neck. "I'm so sorry about your truck," she mumbled against his neck.

"Forget the damn truck." His grip around her waist tightened as he pulled her close. All he cared about was her. She might mess with his head like no other woman could but the thought of Eve hurt...he shuddered. Lightly, he stroked his hand down her back, hoping to soothe her. Though he hated to do it, he slightly pulled back to look at her. Mascara smudged under her eyes and blood had dried on her forehead but she seemed to focus on him without any trouble. "Are you okay? What happened?"

Before she could respond the two EMTs appeared out of nowhere barking orders. He understood he needed to move and let them take care of her, but the most primal part of him didn't want to leave her side for even a second.

Feeling helpless, he stepped back as they helped Eve to her feet. "I'll follow you to the hospital."

"But your truck..."

He shook his head. He didn't give a shit about that. "Don't worry about that. I'll see you in a little bit."

With watery eyes, she nodded as the two men helped her stand and put her on the stretcher. Since she was moving on her own he doubted she even needed it but he was glad they weren't taking any chances.

Once she was out of earshot he turned to the two ranchers. He nodded politely at them but didn't bother with small talk. "DJ, Derek. What the hell happened?"

Derek took off his hat and shook his head. "Don't know exactly. Saw a dark SUV run her off the road. I think the driver started to slow down until they saw us coming from the other direction. We thought it was you in the truck at first until we got to the accident."

He frowned at their words. "Was it intentional?"

The two men glanced at each other, then Derek nodded. "I think so. It could have been someone passing through being an asshole but it didn't seem that way. I got part of the license plate at least."

As the sound of a siren grew louder, Mac glanced over his shoulder. Sheriff Marcel was pulling up. Mac quickly looked at Derek. "Can I see what you wrote down?" He wanted to look at it before the sheriff took it.

Derek nodded and handed it to him. He memorized the few numbers and letters before giving it back. Mac wasn't sure what was going on, but if someone had intentionally tried to hurt Eve, they were going to pay.

CHAPTER SIX

After dealing with the tow truck company and talking to the sheriff, Mac managed to get away from the scene. All he wanted to do was check on Eve at the hospital. The sheriff would be on his way there soon to question her and he wanted to arrive first. He'd rescued her phone from the cabin of his truck so he didn't have a way to contact her until he saw her.

From what he could tell she'd looked fine but his truck was totaled—and it wrecked him that she'd been driving the mangled mess.

"I've never seen you like this, man." Griffin shook his head as he headed toward downtown.

"What do you expect? My truck's totaled," he growled at him.

Griffin snorted. "This has nothing to do with that truck and everything to do with one very petite, very cute blonde."

"It's strawberry blonde," he muttered, not sure why the distinction mattered. But it did. Everything about Eve mattered.

At that Griffin laughed, but Mac ignored him. "I don't know why you don't get it over with and ask her out."

"Are you still talking?" He and Griffin had been in the Marines together and he loved him like a brother but right now, he didn't want to hear it. He just wanted to make sure Eve was okay.

"Well if you're not interested, maybe I'll ask her out myself."

"Do it and I kick your ass," he growled softly without looking at him.

Griffin laughed again so Mac kept his mouth shut. He didn't feel like being baited and that's all his friend was doing.

The rest of the drive to the hospital was quiet and thankfully short. Without having to tell Griffin to drop him off at the ER entrance, his friend pulled through and stopped.

"I'll park and meet you inside."

"Okay." He jumped out and hurried to the entrance. As he was walking through, Eve was walking out. She jerked to a stop when she spotted him. "Uh, hey."

"Are you leaving?" he demanded.

Her hair was pulled back in a ponytail and other than the small bandage on her forehead, she actually looked okay. She must have washed her face because she didn't have a scrap of makeup on and all the smudged mascara was gone. She nodded as her cheeks tinged bright pink. "I can't stay here and I'm fine."

While he wanted to hug and protect her, he simultaneously wanted to throttle her. "How were you planning on leaving?"

She bit her bottom lip. "Um..."

"Damn it, Eve, you never think things through. You don't have your car or a phone." He fished hers out and handed it to her. "And you need to make a statement to the sheriff. He's on his way here now. I know you were run off the road intentionally and so does he. What the hell is going on? I know this wasn't an accident."

"I honestly don't know. I went to see Bunny Martin and—"

"You *what?*"

Her lips pulled into a thin line. "I didn't tell her anything and according to her she's leaving her husband. Though I guess that doesn't matter now...Anyway, she gave me his phone records for the past few months and—"

"Why the hell did she do that?" He couldn't stop interrupting her.

Her shoulders slumped. "Look, I'm hungry and I feel like crap. Can you take me to Brick's Diner? I'm starving and I promise I'll call the sheriff on the way there. I'll stop by the station as soon we leave."

Stubborn woman was in no shape to be going anywhere. "You need to stay here, Eve. After what happened—"

She shook her head and wrapped her arms around herself. "I'm scared to stay here!"

His eyebrows rose at the raw terror in her voice. "Are you serious?"

She nodded, eyes haunted. "Whoever ran me off the road must have been following me or something. They know I'll be here and it's not that I don't trust Hudson Creek P.D., but..."

"But you *don't* trust them."

"Well, what if the sheriff doesn't believe me? I haven't exactly been truthful with him and here I'm a sitting duck. *Please*, I don't want to stay."

The pleading note in her voice did him in. Well, that and the way she looked at him with those big brown eyes.

Sucker. That's exactly what he was. A big one. Knowing he was going to regret his decision, he shook his head and put a protective arm around her shoulders. "Come on. Griffin's parking the truck."

* * *

Oscar Perez tightly gripped the wheel of the SUV. He wasn't sure what the nosy little journalist knew, but she had to know something. Why else would she have stopped by Allen Martin's house? He'd been randomly staking out Martin's residence for the past few months. The car salesman had been acting odd lately and their operation was too big to risk him getting cold feet and bailing. And the reporter woman had *never* stopped by before.

Maybe Allen had talked to her before he'd died... No, he'd been neck deep in their operation. He wouldn't have contacted a journalist.

After glancing in the rearview mirror to make sure he wasn't being followed, Oscar pulled out his cell phone.

His contact answered on the second ring and she sounded annoyed. "What's wrong? We're not supposed to be in communication today."

Rolling his eyes, he shook his head. He'd set up the schedule. "I saw that blonde journalist, Eve Newman, leaving Martin's house. She talked with his wife for a while."

"What did they talk about?"

"Hell if I know." He hadn't been in the room. "I ran her off the road after she left. Thought I'd be able to intimidate her into telling me what she knows, but I didn't get a chance to question her. Someone stopped to help her."

She sighed loudly, which only made him grit his teeth. "She's a nosy little bitch. Did you kill her?"

"I don't think so."

"Then she's probably at the hospital. I can't risk running into her there but you should stop by. I'm sure you can *convince* her to talk to you."

He didn't like the idea of going to the hospital and exposing himself like that. Especially not when they were so close to bringing in more money than he'd ever dreamed of. Cops would likely be at the hospital and he didn't exactly fit in there. "The hospital is too public. I'll wait until she's released."

"That's fine. I actually have a better idea. I'd planned to use it on Allen but I can use it on her instead." She sounded a little too excited.

He knew exactly what she meant and the idea was stupid. "That will bring too much heat down on us and we're not even sure if she knows anything yet."

"Someone saw Allen's body last night and we were lucky enough to clean up the blood before that patrolman showed up. If he'd looked around a little harder..." She trailed off and he could picture her tapping her fingers against her desk. "Well, whatever. If Eve was there, I don't think she saw us or she'd have told the cops. But if she keeps nosing around, she might figure something out. This needs to be done immediately."

This was going to be violent and explosive. Normally he didn't mind a little violence but right now he wanted to play things safe. Fly under the radar. But arguing was stupid. She would do it anyway because she liked to push boundaries. He'd only gone into business with her because she'd been able to help him make contacts he otherwise wouldn't have. And he'd bought into her dumb routine too easily.

She was anything but stupid. Sharp and savvy most of the time, she expertly pushed his product and kept people coming back for more. But she got too excited sometimes and tended to act rashly. "Fine. Get rid of her but keep it contained to *only* her. I don't want anyone else hurt or involved."

She muttered something then hung up.

Something Oscar wouldn't tolerate from anyone else. And one day soon he wouldn't tolerate it from her either. He planned to build his own empire and she was a stepping stone.

CHAPTER SEVEN

Eve knew Mac was annoyed with her but after she'd called the sheriff, he'd settled down. Well, sort of. There was still an edginess about him. He'd been quiet at lunch, just giving her hooded stares that made her blood heat up and only served to confuse her. She shifted in the back seat of Griffin's truck as he drove them to her place.

"Whatever your insurance doesn't cover, I'll pay for," she said, mainly to break the silence. Since leaving the diner, he'd agreed to let her get her car. But he didn't seem too happy about it. It's not like she had a concussion. Sure she was achy and her neck hurt but she was fine to drive. And if she went home now and took the nap that her body craved, she wouldn't be able to follow up on her lead. She was obviously on to something and truth be told, she was scared to be home alone anyway.

"Enough with the damn truck." He didn't turn around to look at her.

"Then what's the matter with you? You were moody all through lunch," she snapped.

Griffin cleared his throat from the driver's side, as if reminding them he was there. But she didn't care.

Mac whipped around in his seat. "*You're* what's the matter with me. You should still be in the hospital. Or talking to the sheriff right now. At the very least you should be at home resting!"

"I am going to talk to the sheriff, but I need my car." Since the sheriff had the partial license plate already he'd been pretty accommodating in letting her come in later.

"Someone tried to hurt you, maybe even kill you, a few hours ago. You should be more concerned."

"I *am* concerned." Actually, she was *terrified*, but that only meant she needed to figure out who was after her that much faster. And she couldn't trust the cops to do it for her. She could only depend on herself for this and she didn't want to drag Mac into whatever mess this was.

He muttered something under his breath, then said, "I'm driving you to the sheriff's station."

"I'm more than capable of taking myself and you need to go to work anyway." Now he was starting to put her on edge.

"Don't tell me what I need to do." His voice was a low growl.

"Then don't tell me you're going to be chauffeuring me around like I'm incapable." She wasn't sure why she was arguing with him. The thought of him staying with her was nice but she didn't like his whole bossy attitude.

"I've got your keys so deal with it." He turned around in his seat, effectively cutting her off.

Frowning, she patted her jacket pocket and then looked in her purse. She couldn't remember where she'd put her car keys this morning but she'd probably left them in her purse after locking up her house. She wasn't sure when he'd managed to snag them though. Maybe when she'd gone to the restroom at lunch. Which meant he'd been expecting an argument from her.

She scowled at the back of his head but didn't say anything else. She knew when to pick her battles. After they pulled up to her place, Mac jumped out and opened the extended cab door for her.

His expression softened as he helped her out and she pushed down the guilt she experienced for fighting with him. He also didn't let go of her hand as they stood there. "I don't want to fight with you. Are you sure you're okay to head to the station?"

She nodded and decided to keep it to herself that she planned to head to her office afterward. He really wouldn't like that. And after the way he'd raced down to the accident site to check on her...she wasn't quite sure what to make of that. "I promise I'm fine. And I'm sorry...well, for everything."

He nodded then looked over at Griffin. "Did you see anyone follow us?"

Follow them? Before she could ask what he meant, Griffin said, "No. But I'll still tail you to the station."

"What are you talking about?" she asked as they headed to her parked car.

"Someone wanted to hurt you today and I made sure they didn't follow us from the hospital or the diner. After what happened last night you and I both know that probably has something to do with today. You need to tell Sheriff Marcel. He can help you in ways I can't."

She snorted.

"Damn it, Eve. He's not—"

"Please don't say his name," she murmured.

Because it was her and because she'd had a rough day, Mac shut his mouth even though every instinct inside him told him to argue with her until she conceded. She headed for the passenger side, which said a lot about how bad she was feeling. She wasn't even trying to argue with him again.

As he got into the front seat, he glanced at her to find her clutching her purse possessively in her lap. No doubt protecting those phone records she'd gotten. Sighing, he slid the key into the ignition and turned the engine over. When it clicked, he frowned. "Have you had any problems with your battery?"

"No. I just got a new one."

The hairs on the back of his head tingled. A feeling he'd never ignored before. "Get out now!"

With wide eyes, she didn't question him. She grabbed her handle and yanked the door open before jumping out.

He did the same and ran.

A deafening blast ripped through the air. Heat licked at his back as he felt himself being lifted off the ground. The only thing he could think of was Eve as he flew through the air.

With a thud, he landed chest down on a patch of grass. All the air rushed from his lungs at the impact. He covered his head at the sounds of glass shattering. When her bumper slammed into the ground next to him, ripping out a chunk of grass and dirt, he pushed up and stumbled a few more feet, trying to stay out of the line of fire. His knees buckled and he hit the ground.

His ears rang as he tried to move again but he couldn't gain his balance. When he felt a hand on his shoulder, he rolled over ready to fight until he saw Griffin's anxious face.

"Are you all right?" Griffin sounded like he was talking from a mile away.

Mac shook his head, trying to clear it, but it was no use. He tried to push up but his world spun. As he stared at the burning car, his heart dropped.

Eve!

CHAPTER EIGHT

E ve felt like someone had shaken her until her bones rattled. She tentatively opened her eyes and realized she was face down in the grass. She'd jumped from the car like Mac had told her and then tried to run. She didn't think she'd gotten very far though.

All she remembered was a loud explosion then the sensation of being lifted through the air as a smoldering heat lapped at her back. Stretching out one arm, she tested her strength and pushed up. There was a slight buzzing in her ears. Almost like a phone ringing from a long distance.

She was shaking but at least she could move. More than anything she needed to find Mac and make sure he was okay.

As she started to sit up, two strong arms lifted her under her armpits from behind. "I've got you." Mac's steady voice had never sounded so wonderful.

A second later she was sitting on the ground and he was crouched next to her. "Are you all right?"

She managed a slight nod. "I think so."

"Stretch out your arms and move them." After she did what he said, he instructed her to do the same with her legs. Then he made her take a couple deep breaths and tested her ribs for pain. She was sore, like she'd run a marathon or something, but she didn't feel broken. When she did everything he said, he pushed out a sigh of relief.

Eve blinked a couple times as she tried to focus on his face. For a moment he was blurry but cleared up when she shook her head. Someone had tried to kill her. And Mac could've been killed too. That thought alone made her see red. "Are you okay? Did you get hit with any flying debris?"

"I'm fine." He brushed her questions away as if she hadn't spoken. The muscles in his jaw stood out. "You're going to sit here and wait for the ambulance and the sheriff. When Sheriff Marcel gets here you're going to answer every damn question he has for you. You have to tell him what you saw last night."

He spoke to her as if she was a child and she didn't blame him. Maybe she should have told the sheriff earlier but she couldn't go back and change that now. "Okay."

The tension in his face melted into shock. "You...wait, okay? You're not arguing with me?" He arched a dark eyebrow.

"Someone tried to blow me up." She might not like or even trust the local police department, but she couldn't hide the fact that someone had tried to kill her—and almost killed someone she cared about in the process. "I'm sorry I dragged you into all this. If you'd gotten hurt..." Her voice broke off as her throat tightened unexpectedly. If she could go back she'd have never stopped by Mac's place last night. Unfortunately he was the first person she'd thought of because she'd known he'd help her. Now he was paying for her mistake.

"I'm not." He reached out and brushed the pad of his thumb across her cheek. Probably to wipe off some dirt or grass but she liked the way his touch felt. Way too much.

"Mac..." Staring at his lips she leaned in closer. He could provide the kind of strength she desperately needed right now. The ringing in her ears was gone but she was suddenly hot all over. His blue eyes darkened to something she'd only seen a glimpse of last night. A sound rumbled deep in his throat as he moved forward.

"Sheriff is pulling down your street. You sure you're okay, Eve?" Griffin hurried toward them holding his cell phone.

His question jerked her back to reality and away from Mac's touch. That's when she heard it. Sirens. For the second time today. "I think I'm okay." Holding out her hand to Mac, she let him pull her to her feet, but she didn't let go right away. The sensation of his callused hands on hers sent a strange tingling sensation down her spine.

When she swayed, he put an arm around her shoulder and let her use him for support. His spicy, masculine scent wrapped around her like a warm, comforting blanket, almost making her forget what had happened.

As she focused on what was left of her smoldering car, bile rose in her stomach. The front doors were blown off, all the glass was shattered and the two front seats were practically obliterated. Dancing embers flickered across the remains. "Holy shit." She and Mac could have been in there. When unexpected tears pricked her eyes, she tried to turn away but he pulled her tighter and murmured soothing sounds against her hair. Not caring what anyone thought, she buried her face against his chest. She was so glad he was with her now.

She almost never cried and today she couldn't seem to shut off the waterworks. When she finally got her control back, she drew away from him. "Can we sit down somewhere?" *Away from the wreckage.* She didn't say it but she knew he'd understand. She wasn't nauseous but her knees were weak.

As he started to help her toward his truck, the sheriff, three patrol cars and an ambulance all screeched to a halt in front of her house, blocking half the street.

Sheriff Marcel was out first. Concern filled his expression as he hurried toward them. "What the hell happened? Are you two okay?"

"Someone blew up Eve's car." She was thankful Mac answered for her.

The sheriff eyed her cautiously. "Does this have anything to do with your 'accident' earlier today?" He didn't sound exactly sarcastic—probably because she'd almost died—but he obviously knew she'd been holding something back from him.

She nodded. "I think so."

Two male paramedics—different than the ones who'd helped her earlier—quickly descended on her and Mac.

As the men steered them toward the back of the ambulance, the sheriff followed them. "What's going on?"

"I'll tell you everything, but..." She nodded at the two paramedics. "Not around anyone else."

He gritted his teeth before turning to one of his patrolmen and barking out orders to cordon off the explosion site. He also told everyone to stay away from her house. From the sound of it, he'd called in a bomb squad from the next county and they were going to check her house before anyone entered it.

Smart, she thought hazily. Her head began to pound as one of the paramedics helped her into the back of the ambulance. After she answered a dozen questions geared toward making sure she didn't have a concussion, he checked her completely over but other than the gash she'd gotten from the car accident earlier, she was fine. Sore everywhere and definitely shaken up, but she refused his insistence to take her to the hospital. It would be pointless and they couldn't make her go. From her eavesdropping of Mac's conversation with the other man, he wasn't going either.

Once they were finished, the sheriff guided them toward his car and away from everyone else. She leaned against the back door for support.

"What have you gotten yourself into, Eve?"

She bristled at his question. This wasn't her fault. Well, maybe some of it was but she hadn't asked to be almost blown up. "You know that anonymous call you received last night?"

His eyes narrowed as he nodded.

Suddenly she lost some of her steam. She cleared her throat. "Hypothetically, let's say it was me who called. Let's say I received an anonymous email advising me to head to the Underwood mansion for a good story. When I got there, I might have—hypothetically—seen Allen Martin's dead body in the pool house."

He swore softly but Mac stepped closer and put an arm around her shoulders. The silent show of support made her stomach flip-flop.

Finally Sheriff Marcel spoke. "Did you see who did it?"

"No, I...you believe me?" Her eyebrows rose.

He nodded. "Yeah. Despite what you might think, we follow up on leads. Martin hasn't been to work in a few

KILLER SECRETS | 75

days and while that isn't exactly odd, the call came from his cell phone and it's been turned off ever since. No one has seen him, not even his wife. Right now I'm working on getting a warrant to search the DA's pool house."

"Martin's wife is leaving him, so..." Eve trailed off as she realized what she was admitting.

"How do *you* know?"

She sighed. Might as well admit it now. "I went to see her today."

He swore again but didn't look surprised. "Before or after someone tried to run you off the road?"

"Before."

"Damn it, Eve—"

"If you believed me at the station, why didn't you tell me?"

"You're a journalist." He said it so clear cut, as if the reason should be obvious.

Which in hindsight, it was. He'd never been very forthcoming with her. Still, it annoyed her. "Do you think the DA is involved?"

"I'm not going to discuss any more details of this case with you. I will need you to make an official statement and after this I'm putting you in protective custody until we figure out what the hell is going on. And where is Martin's phone anyway?" He spouted off everything with machine gun fire speed.

She stepped closer into Mac's embrace. Not because he happened to be there, but because it was him. The man who'd been there for her too many times to count. Even when they'd been kids. When she was eight and he'd been ten, she'd broken her arm on his father's ranch after falling off a horse. He'd helped her back to the house and hadn't made fun of her for crying. Unlike her brother who'd teased her mercilessly. Not Mac though.

When she realized the sheriff was staring at her, she felt her cheeks redden. "I'll make a statement but I don't have Martin's phone. After I took it..." She glanced at Mac who nodded for her to continue. When she looked back at the sheriff, she cringed. He was so not going to be happy with her. "After I took it, someone chased me and shot at me. I didn't see his face but I heard his voice. He had a Spanish accent, that's the only thing I know for sure. I ran and ditched the phone, but I did take the SIM card out of it before I got rid of it. I doubt you'll need it since you can probably subpoena Martin's records but I swear I was going to give it to you guys."

"She was." Mac's deep voice cut through the conversation, causing both of them to look at him. "And she wanted to tell you everything but I wasn't sure that was the smartest idea. I didn't want her to become a target, but it looks like it doesn't matter anyway. Someone knows she saw something."

Her mouth fell open at his blatant lie but she quickly shut it. She wasn't sure why he was lying to protect her. She'd be responsible for withholding evidence if the sheriff decided to prosecute her either way.

Sheriff Marcel sighed and scrubbed a hand over his face. "I don't care why you withheld this info. I'm not going to bring charges against you only because I know you're not involved in this and I understand why you held back. But remember I am *not* my predecessor," he said, as if reading her mind. "Where's that SIM card now?"

She fished it out of her purse and handed it to him. She didn't tell him she'd made a copy of it and she didn't say anything about the phone records she'd gotten from Bunny. The cops would be able to get those records easily—and they probably already had them. Just because he believed her didn't mean she was going to stop investigating this story. Someone had tried to kill her twice and Mac had almost gotten killed in the process. She wasn't going to let that slide. "Thank you for everything, Sheriff, but I'm not going into protective custody."

He started to argue when Mac interrupted him. "She'll be staying with me. The ranch is about as secure as anything. I've got guys patrolling 24/7 so I'll increase my numbers." When the sheriff tried to interrupt again, Mac shook his head. "I'm not letting Eve out of my sight, so save it. You could try forcing the issue but you and I both know what she's like. You won't be able to keep her anywhere for long. It'll be a waste of manpower I'm sure you don't have. Keeping her with me will be better."

Eve gritted her teeth that he talked about her like she wasn't even there but she was grateful when the sheriff finally nodded. "Damn it, you're right. Do me a favor Eve and don't harass the DA, okay?"

"So you *do* think he's involved?" His non-answer earlier had been a giveaway but she wanted to hear him say it.

He shook his head. "I didn't say that. Just…stay out of trouble and keep a low profile. If I find out you're not staying under lockdown with Mac I'll lock you up myself."

She wasn't sure if he meant it or not so she bit back a response and nodded. "Okay."

CHAPTER NINE

Mac pulled Eve's suitcase from the back of Griffin's truck. After the bomb squad had cleared her house, she'd packed a bag and they'd headed to the police station to make a statement. That had taken another hour and a half.

Dusk had already fallen and he was beat. More mentally than anything. But at least Eve was alive and unharmed. He'd nearly lost a decade of his life during those moments he hadn't known if she'd been all right.

When he'd found her lying face down in the grass, he could have sworn his heart stopped beating. Until she'd moved. Then something foreign had twisted inside him. Something he didn't want to admit existed for her. That sharp burst of adrenaline and the need to protect her had nearly overwhelmed him. That need had always been there. Since they were kids in fact. But this was different. It wasn't simply a need to keep her safe. He wanted to claim her so that every male in the damn state knew she belonged to him.

After Griffin headed toward the bunkhouse where he stayed during the weeks he was on night rotation at the ranch, Eve cleared her throat nervously. "I never got a chance to ask you, but why'd you lie to the sheriff?"

"What are you talking about?" Enough hours had passed that he'd hoped she'd forget about it. Should have known better. The woman forgot *nothing*.

"When you told him you convinced me not to tell the police about what I'd seen."

He shrugged as they reached his front door. "I didn't want you to get in any trouble."

"I don't need a big brother." She sounded testy and he wasn't sure why.

He sure as hell didn't have *brotherly* feelings for her. After last night she should know that. "And I don't want to be your brother," he muttered. He wished that was all he wanted. Sleeping under the same roof would be a hell of a lot easier if his feelings were platonic. He might not *want* to want her, but that burning deep-seated need for her wasn't going away any time soon. The longer he was around her, the more obvious that became.

She said something he couldn't understand but he wasn't going to ask her to repeat it. He wanted a cold beer and a hot shower. "Which room do you want?" he asked as they reached the beginning of the hallway.

Eve took the bag from his hand. "I'll stay in the one I did last night if that's all right?"

He'd rather her sleep in his bed. He told himself it was simply because he wanted to hold her. To convince himself she was okay. But that was bullshit. He wanted to bury himself inside her and make her come so many times she didn't remember the touch of anyone before him. The offer was on the tip of his tongue but somehow he reined it in. Damn, he really did need sleep. "It's fine. I'm going to grab a beer."

She nodded. "I'll be there in a sec."

For a moment he watched the sway of her ass as she strode down the hallway. What he wouldn't give to slide his hands down her back and cup that perfection. The woman was soft and curvy in all the right places. Just once he wanted to feel all that womanly softness pressed up against him when she was stripped bare to him. No clothes, no barriers and the only thing in her eyes would be desire and heat.

He shook himself out of his trance and headed for the kitchen. Eyeing the contents of his stainless steel fridge, he frowned. There wasn't much there. The men who lived on the land ate supper at his house during the week but they always took the leftovers back to the fridge in the bunkhouse.

"Got any beer for me?" He turned at the sound of Eve's voice.

"Yeah." He grabbed two and handed her one. "I don't have much food but you're free to take a look." As he popped the top of his bottle he tried not to stare too hard. She'd taken off her boots and jacket and looked very comfortable and at ease in his home. Where he wouldn't mind her spending more time.

"This is perfect." She leaned against the counter and sighed happily after she'd taken a long pull from the bottle.

His eyes narrowed on her mouth again. Full, lush lips he'd finally got to taste last night. After years of wondering what she'd be like, he'd found out she was as responsive as he'd hoped. Now he wanted more. He didn't care that they would likely never work in the long term. His cock pushed against his zipper as he watched her take another pull then move the bottle away. When those sexy lips pulled into a thin line he realized he was staring a little too hard.

Immediately he averted his gaze and met her dark eyes. She arched a blonde eyebrow but didn't say anything. The heat he saw in her gaze made him ache with raw need. Screw the long term worries. He'd almost lost her today. Blindly, he set his beer down behind him and took a step toward her. When he did, her eyes widened a fraction but she didn't make a move to leave.

After the way she'd run out on him last night his inner voice told him this was a stupid idea, but around her all he seemed to have were stupid ideas. Lying to the police for her and letting her stay with him were a recipe for disaster.

In the end he knew he'd get burned by feisty Eve Newman. It was hard to care when she was staring at him with those big brown eyes that begged him to throw her over his shoulder, take her to his bedroom and not come out for hours. Days even.

The closer he got he realized she was covering the distance from her end. He didn't even remember moving, but suddenly their mouths clashed. She let out a heated moan and wrapped her hands around the back of his neck.

Something about her brought out his most primal side. He didn't quite understand it and whatever it was, it made him want to dominate yet protect the little vixen with a fierceness that stunned him.

As her tongue stroked against his in erotic teasing flicks, one of her hands slid down his chest and didn't stop until she grasped his erection through his jeans. His hips jerked against her touch. Too much clothing was in the way. What he wouldn't give to feel her hand—or mouth—on him.

His hands tightened around her hips and he started walking them back toward the center island. Holding on to her, he lifted her up and placed her on the counter. As he did, she cried out, but it wasn't from desire.

Drawing back, he opened his eyes. "Are you okay?"

She nodded, her eyes still hazy and lusty. "I'm fine. I guess I'm more sore than I realized." Her voice had that sexy, breathy quality that made his cock jump to attention. Not that it mattered right now.

He sighed and leaned forward until their foreheads touched. Nothing was going to happen between them tonight. Not with the way he felt. He couldn't be gentle or tender and that's exactly what she needed. After an accident, then almost being blown up, she would be sore for a couple days. And he wasn't going to hurt her further by pushing things tonight.

"I think we should call it a night." He barely recognized the raspy growl of his own voice.

She bit her bottom lip and for a moment it looked like she was going to say no, but she eventually nodded. "Yeah. You're probably right."

As he drew back and helped her off the counter, he tried to shift but it only enflamed his cock more. "Stay with me tonight." The words slipped out before he could stop himself. "Not for...anything physical, but stay with me. That way I'll know you're safe."

Her cheeks tinged an adorable shade of pink. "Okay." She almost seemed shy as she agreed. Nothing about her was timid but he liked that he obviously affected her as much as she affected him.

He threw an arm around her shoulder as they made their way back to his room, but she paused at the entrance.

"I'm going to take a shower and change," she murmured.

"Okay." He didn't say anything else. Instead he let his arm drop. He was afraid he'd pull her into his arms again if he kept touching her.

After changing, he slipped into bed and stared at his ceiling, counting the seconds until she joined him. Even though he knew it would be torture being able to hold her but not do anything else, it was something he'd gladly sign up for anytime.

When Eve paused in his doorway, his entire body tensed. She'd changed into completely respectable pajamas that unfortunately covered her arms, legs and everything in between.

Her strawberry blonde hair was damp and hanging loose around her face. "Are you sure you want me to sleep with you?" Her voice was hesitant and totally out of character.

Since he didn't trust his voice, he pulled back the covers on the other side of the bed. Wordlessly she hurried over and slid in. Feeling like a randy teenager completely out of his depth, he wrapped his arm around her waist and pulled her to his chest. His hand settled over her stomach and he forced himself to keep it there even though the urge to move higher and cup her breast was strong.

Sighing deeply, she snuggled back against him, then froze. She wiggled once, right over his erection, then paused again. "Uh, Mac?"

"Go to sleep." He knew he wouldn't be sleeping anytime soon but it was worth the torture.

"Are you sure—"

"Get some rest," he murmured in her ear.

It was slight but he felt her tremble in his hold. In a day or two, things would be different between them. He could feel it straight to his core. Hell, things already *were* different than a week ago. This was the first step. Even though holding her like this made his craving for her worse and even though it would kill him when things ended between them, nothing could get rid of this ache. Nothing but Eve.

CHAPTER TEN

Eve dropped her stack of papers on Mac's kitchen table, turned on her laptop, then went in search of coffee. It was almost noon, which surprised her. She couldn't remember the last time she'd slept so hard and so late. And it was all because of Mac. They might not have gotten physical but she'd felt completely safe in his strong embrace.

She had a voicemail from her boss telling her she better not come in to work today and to keep her head down. He'd heard about the explosion and from the sound of it, he wasn't happy she hadn't called him about it. Apparently Sheriff Marcel had let him know a little about what was going on and made it clear she was supposed to be under lockdown. Fine with her. She might not be headed to work but that didn't mean she wouldn't be following up on this story. At least she wouldn't have Mac around as a distraction. He was a good distraction of course, but right now she needed to focus. With him around, all she wanted to focus on was his hot body.

He'd woken around dawn and had let her know he'd be heading out, but that he was available by cell and had two of his guys watching the house. If Mac trusted the men then she did too.

Before he'd left he'd looked like he wanted to say more but she'd been too tired to press him. The conversation she wanted to have with him wasn't an early morning kind anyway. After that kiss and the gentle way he'd held her last night, she was even more confused and wasn't sure what she should be feeling. The feel of his erection pressing against her back had been unmistakable and he hadn't tried to hide it. Nope, he'd been content to hold her.

Shaking those thoughts free because they'd only distract her, she started a pot of coffee and went back to the table. First, she cross-referenced the numbers from Martin's SIM card and the call log. The ones that weren't on the call log, she disregarded for the moment. If he hadn't called a number in the past three months, it could wait. Out of the almost two dozen numbers that he'd called with a decent amount of frequency, three were called with a surprising regularity and at odd hours. She highlighted the three numbers and the call times.

The one with the most calls was the number she called first. According to his SIM card, it belonged to a Beth Woods.

A woman answered on the first ring. "Hello?" She sounded out of breath and nervous.

"Beth Woods?" Eve asked.

"Yes. Who is this?"

Eve hadn't used her personal cell phone, but a backup she used when working on stories. "My name is Eve Newman. I'm calling about Allen Martin and—"

"Is he hurt? Where is he? I need to see him." Her voice was frantic and it was obvious her interest was personal.

"When was the last time you saw him?"

"A week ago...why are you asking me that? Wait, *Eve Newman*, I recognize your name. You work for the Hudson Creek Gazette don't you?"

"Yes. I was wondering if—"

"Do you know something about Allen? He hasn't called or stopped by in days and that's not like him. We had plans last night and..." She broke off and started softly crying. "Something must have happened to him. I just know it."

"You're sleeping with him," Eve said softly. Immediately she wished she could take the comment back. She hadn't meant to come off as callous but it had slipped out. If Martin's wife was correct, this was probably one of the women he'd been seeing. Considering the number of times he'd called this woman, it was definitely more than casual.

"It's more than that. We love each other. Why are you calling me? Has something happened to him? Why aren't the police involved?"

"I don't know that anything has happened to Mr. Martin." She swallowed the lie. This was her job and finding out the identity of Allen Martin's murderer was important. "I'm simply following up on a lead for a story so if you have any information about him you think might be important—"

"I don't know anything! If something has happened to him you should be calling the police, not me. Why aren't you questioning his wife? He was leaving her for me. Maybe she did something to him." Her voice rose with each word, nearing hysteria.

"Thank you for your time, Ms. Woods. I'm sorry to have bothered you." She ended the call and sighed in a combination of irritation and guilt.

It was obvious Martin and Bunny were headed for divorce court, but why would Bunny kill him at the Underwood mansion? And who was the man she'd heard that night? Eve was usually a pretty good judge of character and his wife hadn't seemed homicidal. No, she'd appeared almost relieved to be rid of him. And it was pretty obvious Beth didn't know anything. While Eve felt bad she hadn't been able to tell the woman her lover was dead, that was the least of her worries. Finding Martin's killer and her would-be killer was the most important thing right now.

Next she called the other two numbers on the call log but they both went to an automated voicemail after a few rings. After tallying up the next batch of the most-called numbers she discovered one was his lawyer and the other his bank. She marked those off. The third was supposedly the DA's house. When Betsy Underwood—the DA's wife—answered, she immediately hung up. She'd only called to clarify it was the right number and now she knew for certain. Even if she wanted to talk to her, she had nothing to say. For a brief moment she thought about calling the sheriff but knew it wouldn't do any good. She didn't have proof of anything. Sure, she had proof he'd called the DA a lot. Which meant they were friends. Big deal.

While she felt slight elation at Martin and the DA's connection, it was tiny and short-lived. All she knew was that they talked on the phone at odd hours. She didn't know why Martin was dead or what he'd been involved in to get him killed. She was back to square one. Hell, she'd never really left it.

After she organized her notes, she pulled up another article on her laptop that she'd started on the upcoming parade next month. Not exactly riveting stuff but she had to do something. If not, she'd go stir-crazy stuck in Mac's house. She couldn't go to work and she couldn't go anywhere else unless she wanted to worry about someone trying to kill her.

As she finished the first draft of her article, her cell phone rang. She glanced at the number and frowned. It was Tara Underwood. The DA's daughter. Eve's heart rate quickened as she answered it. "Hey, Tara."

"Hey! How have you been? I heard some craziness about you almost getting yourself blown up. Is it true?" She sounded way too excited and intrigued. Which meant whatever Eve said would be spread like wildfire moments after they got off the phone.

Word traveled too fast in this town. Not that she'd expect anything less from the kind of event yesterday. "Where'd you hear that?"

"*Everyone* is talking about it. My father is in a tizzy trying to get the sheriff to talk to him about it. He wants charges pressed against whoever did this and..." She continued droning on, but Eve frowned.

Yeah, she bet Tara's father really cared about who'd tried to blow her and Mac up. She hadn't talked to Tara in a while and Eve couldn't help but wonder if Tara's father had put the idea in her head to contact Eve.

"... And I hear you and sexy Mac Quinn are a hot item now. Every time I see that man in town I want to jump him, lucky girl. Are you bringing him to the fundraiser tomorrow night?"

Crap. She'd forgotten her boss had given the staff tickets weeks ago for the *Find a Cure for Lymphoma* fundraiser. "I'll be there," she said before she could stop herself. The sheriff might have made her promise not to harass the DA, but he couldn't stop her from attending a public event. The sheriff and Mac were going to be pissed she was going to the fundraiser but she didn't care. She wanted to see the DA's reaction to her and if she got to talk to him, maybe he'd slip up. She wasn't worried about her safety, especially since she'd be dragging Mac along with her. He wouldn't like it but she knew how to convince him otherwise.

Eventually she managed to get off the phone with Tara and when Eve saw how late it was getting, she cleaned up the table and headed back to the guest room. Mac had let her know his cook would be coming in around dusk to prepare the evening meal for the men and she didn't want to get in the way. Smiling to herself, she stripped and jumped in the shower. She might be a little sore from the accident, but things were definitely going to change between her and Mac tonight. She'd had strong feelings for him for over a decade and they obviously weren't going away. If anything they'd only gotten stronger the last couple days.

What she'd been forcefully keeping at bay for so long had bubbled to the surface and she could no longer deny she had completely fallen for Mac. Now that she knew he felt something for her, she wasn't waiting any longer. Even if things ended between them, she couldn't risk not taking a chance.

* * *

Mac was tired, cranky and horny. The cold shower jets pummeling his body weren't doing a damn thing to ease his discomfort. Eve hadn't joined him and his men for dinner—not that he'd exactly expected her—but he hadn't seen her once since he'd gotten home. All day he'd felt anticipation humming through him. At first he'd chalked it up to being worried about the unknown and who was after Eve. But he knew better. He'd been excited to see her. All day he'd been distracted to the point that Griffin had noticed and given him shit for it. Not that he cared about that.

He wanted Eve so bad he ached for it with alarming need. For a moment he wrapped his callused hand around his hard cock and began to stroke. The feel of his rough palm made him wince. He didn't want his hand. He wanted what only Eve could give him.

Sighing, he turned the shower off and stepped out onto the bath mat. After drying off, he didn't bother with clothes. Pulling boxers over his hard cock would only agitate him more.

When he opened the bathroom door and stepped into his bedroom, he froze. Eve was stretched out on his bed, blonde hair framed around her face in seductive waves.

And she was completely naked.

"Hi." She sounded nervous and her cheeks were as pink as her nipples.

He couldn't find his voice. Could only stare. His gaze tracked from her full, lush breasts down the flat planes of her stomach to the juncture between her thighs. Fine, blonde hair covered her mound in a neatly trimmed strip.

His abdomen clenched as he stared. What he wouldn't give to bury his face and cock there. He didn't remember moving but suddenly he was kneeling at the end of the bed. Eve sat up but didn't make a move to cover herself. Her hands were at her side, tightly clutching the covers beneath her.

"Do you want this?" He barely recognized his raspy voice.

She nodded. "Yes."

"Are you nervous?"

She nodded again. "A little."

Hell, he was nervous too. But he wouldn't let anything stop this from happening tonight. She obviously didn't care about talking since she'd come to his room like this. He wasn't a big talker, especially in the bedroom, but at least he could alleviate some of her nerves. All he needed to do was touch her sweet body and show her what she meant to him.

He wanted to take his time but right now his cock throbbed with the demand to be inside Eve. Grasping one of her ankles, he placed a soft kiss to her inner calf. She shuddered lightly and opened her legs farther. It was almost imperceptible but the action wasn't lost on him. She was opening herself up to him.

As he moved his way up her legs, the subtle scent of her desire surrounded him. She smelled like a fresh spring rain. When he reached her inner thighs, he slow-ly kissed and teased above her mound, but never directly stroking her pussy. Her fingers threaded through his hair and she gripped him hard.

It was hard to believe what they were about to do, but there wasn't anywhere else Eve would rather be at that moment. The feel of Mac's lips on her body had turned her into a raging inferno of heat and longing.

Her fingers tightened on his head in a silent plea. She didn't want him to tease her anymore. She wanted to feel that thick length inside her. When he'd walked out of the bathroom with that gorgeous rock hard cock, her inner walls had tightened with the desire to feel him inside her. She appreciated foreplay as much as the next woman but she'd wanted him for too long.

She was tired of being patient.

When he flicked his tongue over her clit, her hips rolled against his face. Such a slight touch and she was ready to combust. He chuckled lightly against the sensi-tive area, which only enflamed her more.

As he teased and stroked her with his tongue, tingles skittered across her entire body. She'd only fantasized about this and now that he was actually doing the things she'd imagined, the real thing was definitely better.

A moan escaped her when he delved his tongue inside her. The graze of his tongue had her legs clenching tighter around his head and her panting harder and harder for relief.

He suddenly pulled back and she froze. Was he going to stop?

"I need to be inside you," he growled softly. His dark eyes were filled with promises she hoped he fulfilled.

Before she could react he grabbed a condom from the nightstand table and quickly ripped it open and sheathed himself. As he rolled it over his cock, her eyes grew heavy-lidded watching him. Next time she planned to do that herself.

Unable to stop herself, she reached out and grasped him. When her fingers closed around his hardness, he made a throaty, almost animalistic sound.

He settled between her spread thighs but placed a hand between their bodies. Covering her mound, he slid a finger inside her. She automatically clamped around him.

"You're so wet," he murmured.

"Please tell me you're going to do something about it." Her voice was playful but she wasn't joking.

The slight trace of humor on his face melted away as he withdrew his hand. Without pause, he thrust inside her.

He filled her completely. Her inner walls molded around him, but before she'd fully adjusted to his size, he pulled out and slammed into her again.

She rolled her hips, meeting him stroke for stroke until their bodies found a sensual, rhythmic dance that had her clawing at his back for release.

When he nipped her earlobe with his teeth, her orgasm slammed into her hard and fast. It was almost unexpected. She knew her body and had thought she was still building to her climax.

Pleasure raced throughout her, sending tingles to all her nerve endings as she rode that high and finally crested into a numb freefall. As her orgasm slowly subsided, Mac's slammed into him with unbridled force.

He groaned loudly in her ear while his once steady thrusts became harder and uncontrolled. Reaching lower, she grabbed on to his butt and dug her nails in. That set him off. Another, more primal sound tore from him until his thrusts slowed and he relaxed and settled on top of her.

Thankfully he used his arms to prop himself up as he stared down at her. His dark eyes glinted possessively. She wasn't sure what the right thing to say was after something like this. Instead of sticking her foot in her mouth like she often did, she reached up and clasped her fingers around his neck.

As she did, he met her mouth and kissed her softly. The tenderness of his tongue stroking over hers was in direct contrast to the hard, fast coupling they'd just had. She sighed in contentment as their tongues continued the sweet, gentle kisses.

Now that she'd been with Mac like this, the fantasies she'd had in the past seemed dull and lifeless. Since she wasn't sure what their future held or even if they had one, she was afraid that if he walked away from her she'd never be able to settle for anything less than him in her bed. He was pretty closed mouth about what he wanted from her and she didn't want to broach the subject. The thought of being that vulnerable to him was too scary.

No, she decided to enjoy what they had without worrying about the future or asking questions she wasn't sure she wanted to know the answer to. When Mac threaded his fingers through her hair and she felt him begin to lengthen inside her again, she knew she'd made the right decision.

Talking and questions could wait until later.

CHAPTER ELEVEN

Mac tugged at his collar and shifted uncomfortably in the driver's seat of his rented car. Eve had somehow convinced him to take her to a fundraiser tonight. The cause might be a good one but he knew that wasn't why she wanted to go. Despite the sheriff's warning, she wanted to see the DA and gauge his reaction to her being there. She hadn't said it in so many words but he knew her well enough by now to know that's what she was up to.

The last place he wanted to take her was anywhere public, but especially not to the Underwood mansion where the fundraiser was being held. After what they'd shared together last night, it was hard to say yes to her when all he wanted to do was lock her up tight and keep the world at bay. At the same time it was also hard to say no to her.

For the briefest of moments last night he'd wondered what she thought of his scarred side but it was almost as if she didn't even see it. All he'd witnessed on her face was lust and need and something else he couldn't put his finger on. Being around her was like a breath of fresh air—even when she was driving him crazy.

He shifted in his seat again and rolled his shoulders. At least it was only semi-formal. Black tie would have been too much. It was bad enough he was wearing a regular suit and tie.

"Stop it. You act like you're escorting me to your own execution," Eve muttered from the passenger seat next to him.

"I don't like this."

"I know. You've only said it a hundred times. It's not like Richard Underwood is going to attack me in front of everyone." She smoothed a hand down her simple black dress, momentarily distracting him.

The strapless gown molded to all her curves and slit up one side to her thigh, revealing too much skin for his taste. He didn't like the thought of anyone else seeing what was his. Barbaric? Totally. He just didn't give a shit.

"It's not like it's a sit down dinner," she continued. "It's cocktails and hors d'oeuvres and a bunch of expensive stuff going up for auction."

Which would be followed by dancing and more mingling. And more time Eve was exposed to whoever wanted her dead. Which was why he didn't plan to let her out of his sight. Not for a moment. Hell, he'd follow her to the restroom if need be. "I don't care. Leave it alone, Eve. I agreed to go."

She mumbled something under her breath about him being a bad date but he ignored it and focused on the road ahead. So far he was sure they hadn't been followed since leaving the ranch. He'd rented a sports sedan so he wouldn't have to take her to the fundraiser in Griffin's truck. He'd also let the sheriff know they were going. The man was livid, not that Mac blamed him. But he'd waited until the last minute to tell the sheriff and there wasn't much the man could do short of taking Eve into custody.

To do that, the sheriff would have to confront her at the fundraiser and Mac didn't see that happening.

They arrived half an hour late so the line of cars wasn't that long. After releasing his car to the valet driver, he headed inside with Eve. A lot of people he recognized, but some he didn't. Their town had grown in the past few years, gaining transplants from some of the bigger cities in Texas.

Most men wore suits and ties though there were a few in tuxedos. All the women wore long gowns and most of them had on too much glittery jewelry that probably cost a fortune. Not Eve. Her hair was pulled back into some sort of complicated twist and she wore simple diamond earrings, but nothing else.

And she looked gorgeous. Frowning as he looked down at her, he realized he hadn't told her. He'd been too pissed she'd roped him into this thing. "You look beautiful," he murmured loud enough for only her as they crossed the threshold into the mansion.

Her head jerked up. Surprise covered her face but was quickly replaced by a megawatt smile. She blushed lightly as she said, "Thanks." When her grip on his arm tightened, he inwardly smiled.

After this thing was over he was going to have her flat on her back again and they wouldn't be leaving his bedroom all weekend if he had any say. Security on his ranch had been ramped up thanks to drug runners trying to smuggle their product across his property and the neighboring one so he might have to make a few runs with his men. But other than that, he planned to spend all his time buried deep inside Eve's tight body.

A giant chandelier hung overhead and to their right was the auction room. From his vantage point, he spotted the DA immediately. Not wanting Eve to see Richard Underwood yet, he stroked his hand down her arm to distract her. He nodded toward the giant room on the left where servers were walking around with trays of champagne and food. "Want to grab a drink?"

Eve nodded absently. "Sure." She didn't care about getting a drink, but knew a small one would probably calm her nerves. She'd thought coming here was the perfect idea and she didn't regret it, but the stark realization that the person who'd tried to kill her might be under the same roof was more than a little frightening. She couldn't help the way she sized up everyone who got too close. Even people she'd known since she was a kid.

An hour and a half later, she still hadn't had a chance to talk to Richard Underwood, but she had seen him. Once the auction had started most small talk had stopped. Now there was a short break in the auction and it was back to mingling for half an hour or so. She'd spotted the DA but he was engrossed in a conversation with the head of one of the local banks and she didn't plan to interrupt him. She could wait him out.

The champagne she'd had earlier had gone right through her. "I need to find a restroom," she whispered to Mac.

Silently, he led them down a hallway with marble floors, custom crown molding and a few paintings she was sure cost more than her house. All from old family money.

She heard female voices inside so when Mac went to open the door, presumably to check out the room, she tugged him back. "I'll be fine," she whispered. She'd been inside years ago and remembered the setup. Two sinks with a giant ornate mirror hanging over them, a settee bench by one wall and the actual toilet and another sink were part of an additional enclosed room. The dark wood plank flooring was a perfect contrast to the rich gold and cream colored hues.

"Be quick or I'm coming in to get you," Mac said before planting a surprisingly heated kiss on her lips.

Before she had time to react, he nudged her toward the door. Her lips tingled from where they'd touched and she was sure anyone could read all the hot thoughts running through her mind. He'd been slightly annoyed all night but he hadn't been paying attention to her at all. Nope, he'd been scanning everyone as a potential threat. The little kiss was a stark reminder of what they'd be doing later that night. Despite her tension, the knowledge of what was to come in a few hours sent a thrill twining through her.

As she entered the large room, a woman she didn't recognize was leaving, but Leslie Gomez was washing her hands at one of the sinks. She hadn't seen the other woman since high school, but she hadn't changed much. Very pretty, petite brunette with dark eyes and perfectly bronzed skin thanks to her Mexican heritage.

When she made eye contact with Eve in the mirror, her eyes widened almost unnaturally. She glanced behind Eve, then breathed out a sigh of relief. "Are you alone?" she whispered.

Eve nodded. She wasn't going to tell her Mac was waiting outside for her. "Yeah."

Leslie glanced in the attached room then stepped back out. "I need to talk to you. In private."

Eve leaned against the counter and crossed her arms over her chest. "*This* is private."

"I was going to try to talk to you after the party, but you're here now and... I sent you that email. I didn't know who else to turn to." She twisted her hands in front of her. "Once I overheard what she was planning I wanted to go to the police, but who would believe me? She's practically royalty around here and her father—"

Eve's heart rate increased. "Slow down. What exactly are you saying?"

Leslie took a deep breath. "I overheard her talking to someone about Allen Martin and from the sound of it, they were going to kill him. I know she's in to some shady stuff but I've never really known what for sure. But I had to tell someone. You were the first person I thought of. The police would never believe my word over hers and I remember how you wrote that story about corruption in the Mayor's office a year ago. I know you're honest and I was hoping you'd be able to help." She picked at the silk material of her dress as she stared expectantly at Eve.

"Who is the woman you're talking about?" Blood rushed loudly in Eve's ears. She figured she already knew the answer from something Leslie had said, but wanted to hear it out loud.

"Tara Underwood," she whispered.

Eve's palms dampened, but she remained still. "Tara? Not her father?" She wanted to deny what Leslie was saying, but how well did she really know Tara? Eve hadn't seen her in years and the woman in front of her had no apparent reason to lie.

Leslie nodded again in that frantic manner. "I haven't been working at her boutique very long, but I've over-heard some strange conversations and I've seen her talk-ing to a very scary man on occasion. Usually later when I'm getting off work he'll be arriving. I don't know if it's drugs or what or even how Allen Martin is involved, but she said he was a problem and that she was going to take care of him. Something about the way she said it..." She shuddered as she trailed off.

"We need to go to the police." Something Eve never thought she'd say with such sincerity.

Leslie shook her head. "I don't know anything."

"Allen Martin is dead and the police are currently running down leads. You need to tell them what you know." Even if Leslie was wrong and Tara wasn't in-volved, they had to tell the police about it. This could be the lead they needed to catch the killer.

Leslie's face paled. "I—"

The door swung open, cutting her off. Eve turned at the sound and nearly stumbled when she saw Tara walk-ing in. Pasting on her game face, she smiled brightly. "Tara. How are you?"

With a thick diamond choker, matching teardrop diamond earrings and a gold shimmery dress, the blonde woman looked stunning. Eve couldn't help but wonder if she'd paid for any of it with illegal money. From what Leslie had said, Eve guessed Tara was definitely into drugs. Dealing or smuggling, she couldn't be sure.

Tara smiled but it looked more like a cougar baring its fangs. "Eve. So glad you were able to make it." She glanced back and forth between Eve and Leslie curiously.

Eve didn't dare turn around. She could only pray that Leslie didn't act nervous or give herself away. When Tara's eyes narrowed at Leslie almost accusingly, Eve knew they were screwed.

It happened so fast, she didn't have time to react. The blonde pulled a snub nose .38 revolver from her clutch purse and pointed it directly at Eve, but directed her attention to Leslie. "You stupid bitch. I wondered how Eve had gotten involved in this. Now I know. I pay you well, give you good benefits and this is how you repay me?"

Behind Eve, Leslie was silent other than a few sniffles that almost sounded like she was crying.

"What are you doing, Tara?" Eve asked, trying to keep the woman's focus away from Leslie. Her heart pounded erratically and sweat bloomed across her forehead, but she didn't dare make a move.

Tara's eyes narrowed dangerously. "You two are going to come with me. The auction is about to start up again and no one will know you're missing."

Mac will. Eve thought it, but didn't say it out loud.

But Tara must have read her mind. "Say a word and I'll kill your boyfriend too," she whispered as she slowly backed toward the door. Keeping the gun trained on them with one hand, she opened the door a fraction. "Mac, sweetie, Eve started her period and I don't have anything. Will you be a doll and go ask one of the servers or better yet, find my mama."

"Uh, Eve?" Mac sounded hesitant.

She hesitated for only a moment. "Hurry up, Mac. I don't have all night." Eve tried not to let her panic show as she spoke. She didn't want Tara to hurt Mac because of her stupidity. On another man the excuse might work but she really hoped Mac wouldn't buy this, even for a female issue.

He sighed heavily. "Give me a few minutes. I'll be right back."

Tara waited a few moments then eased the door open. After peering out, she motioned to them with her gun. "Come on."

"Stay calm," Eve murmured to a trembling Leslie as they exited the room. Her palms dampened even more when she realized Mac wasn't waiting in the hall to ambush Tara. They were alone.

"This way." Tara motioned them in the opposite direction Eve had originally come from.

Following her orders they reached the end of the hallway, made a left and headed for a door that led them into the backyard. They were on the opposite side of the large property from the pool house. Tara dug the gun into her back. "Head for the tennis court."

Eve winced at the slight pain in her back, but didn't say a word. The lights were off and even though she could faintly hear partiers and what was probably some of the valet guys from the front of the house, she didn't dare turn around and look anywhere. Raw fear and the steel digging into her spine was enough to make her cautious of any sudden moves.

"Why'd you kill Allen Martin?" Eve asked quietly. Her heels clicked along the stone patio as they rounded the pool.

"Martin was an idiot. We had a perfect system and he wanted out." She dug the gun in harder and shoved Eve.

When Eve stumbled, Leslie gasped and reached out to help her, but Tara shoved her too. "Don't piss me off anymore, Leslie, and I might make death quick for you."

Eve might not have talked to Tara in a while, but the one thing she knew for certain about the tall blonde was that she liked to talk about herself. So, she decided to fish for information. If she was going to die she wanted to know why. "What would your parents think if they knew what you were doing?"

Tara snorted behind her. "My parents cut me off a year ago so I don't give a damn what they think. My daddy thought he was teaching me a good lesson and it turns out he has taught me something very valuable. There's a whole lot more money in drugs than in a stupid little boutique that barely covers my costs."

Eve's heels sunk into the damp grass as they finished the rest of the trek to the tennis court. She wasn't sure what the woman planned but whatever it was, she and Leslie weren't coming out of this alive unless Mac figured out what was going on in time. She thought about trying to overpower Tara for the weapon, but until she had more leverage she couldn't risk it. If she did, she feared she or Leslie would be shot for sure.

"Where are you taking us?" Eve doubted she'd kill them on the tennis court so she had to have some other sort of plan.

"The same place I took Martin's body. No one will ever find you. Don't worry, I'll be sure to comfort that sexy rancher of yours while he's mourning your disappearance." There was such a malicious edge to her quiet laugh that it sent a shiver slithering down Eve's spine. "Now open it," Tara demanded when they reached the court.

Eve unlatched the green, fenced door and let Leslie walk in first. "Are you going to kill us right here?" She risked a glance over her shoulder to find Tara pulling the door shut behind them.

The woman smirked. "Of course not. Head that way." She motioned to the back left side of the court and that's when Eve saw it. There was a small wooden structure attached to the fenced in area, no doubt a storage shed. "You're going to stay right in here until the fundraiser is over. I'll tell Mac you took poor Leslie home because she was feeling ill. When you two go missing, nothing will point to me. Even if he's suspicious, he'll never be able to pin anything on me. Not with my daddy being the DA."

Eve reined in a snort of derision. Tara obviously didn't know Mac very well. Eve tried to think of any-thing to say to convince the other woman to let them go but knew it was useless. Why would she? She'd caught them and—

"Ahh!" Eve spun around at Tara's sharp exclamation and the sound of a gun clattering to the concrete surface.

She lifted her hands defensively until she saw Mac. He stood over Tara's fallen body, a gun in his hand and a grim expression on his face.

Heart racing, Eve gaped at him. "How did you…"

"I'm not stupid," he said wryly as he picked up Tara's gun. The other woman wasn't moving. "I waited around the corner until she came out with you two and followed. The cops are already on their way. Turns out Sheriff Marcel has already been watching Ms. Underwood on suspicion of transporting illegal narcotics."

Eve glanced at Leslie who'd wrapped her arms around herself and was trembling uncontrollably. Eve's insides were shaky and her knees felt wobbly but she managed to stay calm. After living in a war zone for months on end, having a gun pointed at her sucked, but she'd been in worse situations. "It's okay, Leslie. All you have to do is tell the police what you know. You're fine now."

"I can't believe Tara was really going to kill us. I always thought she was so perfect and..." She trailed off and shook her head but didn't continue as more tears tumbled down her cheeks.

The sound of sirens in the distance made Eve's heart sing. There were still some unanswered questions, like who was the man Eve heard the night she found Allen Martin's body? No doubt it was Tara's partner and something told Eve that as soon as Tara was taken into custody she'd tell the cops everything. She'd be desperate to cut a deal and Eve really hoped the sheriff didn't go easy on her. But more than that, Eve was just happy to be alive. Everything that had happened the past few days was too surreal. Maybe it would all sink in later.

Eve went to Mac and slid her arm around his waist. "Thank you for saving us." The words didn't seem like nearly enough but they would have to do for now.

His entire body was tense as he murmured something she didn't understand against the top of her head. He pulled her into a tight hug and gripped her so tight, it was almost hard to breathe. His strong arms were like steel bands, locking her in with his warmth and strength, both of which she'd gladly take right now.

Sagging against him, she buried her head against his neck, grateful to be alive and safe and in Mac's comforting embrace.

* * *

Oscar sped away from the police station and reviewed his options. He still couldn't believe that bitch Tara had gotten caught. Considering their arrangement, he didn't expect any loyalty from her.

She'd always looked out for herself and had made that perfectly clear from the beginning of their arrangement. He'd needed her because she pushed their product to the wealthy clients of Hudson Creek and with Martin's help they'd been transporting cocaine to various cities around Texas using his vehicles. It had been the perfect arrangement. Three people with almost nothing in common able to make a fortune and fly under the radar while doing so. The fact that Tara's father was the DA had always struck him as ironic. Now it pissed him off. Her father would be sure to let her cut a deal if she flipped on her partner.

If Martin hadn't been so stupid, everything would have been fine. And now Tara was caught. For what, he couldn't be sure, but he did know she wouldn't leave his name out of it for long. After driving to one of his safe houses, he loaded up the pound of coke he'd stashed along with fifty thousand dollars of his emergency money and a couple fake passports.

Always have an exit strategy. Unlike Tara he had few ties to this town. While he didn't want to head to Brownsville, his cousin lived there and could set him up temporarily with a place to live. Brownsville saw too much violence from all the border skirmishes and the law was much tighter there than in Hudson Creek, but it would be a perfect place for him to lay low until he could figure out his next move.

Before he left, he had one more stop. Eve Newman's house. He still wasn't sure if the bitch had seen his face but he couldn't take the chance. If Tara decided to cut a deal and testify against him, he'd take care of her later. But he wasn't going to wait to kill that journalist when he could tie up loose ends now.

CHAPTER TWELVE

Mac glanced in the rearview mirror before switching lanes even though he was fairly certain no one else was on the road at this hour. After dealing with the police, giving their official statement and then making sure Leslie Gomez made it home all right, it was well after two in the morning and he and Eve were dog tired. Instead of driving all the way out to his ranch they'd opted to go to Eve's place. The drive was barely ten minutes but for how he felt it was almost too long.

When he'd seen Tara pointing a gun at Eve he'd gone completely numb. That feeling had quickly morphed into rage though. His fingers tensed around the wheel, digging into the leather. Knocking Tara out and not strangling her was a testament to his self control. If anything had happened to Eve... *No.* She was alive. He looked at her sitting next to him and was able to breathe normally as he was reminded of that fact.

Eve let her head fall back against the headrest and closed her eyes. "I'll be glad when this mess is over."

"Me too," he grunted. Sheriff Marcel had still been questioning Tara when the DA had shown up demanding answers so he and Eve had quickly left the station.

There wasn't anything they could do there anyway and all he wanted right now was to crawl into bed with Eve and hold her tight. He wanted to feel her every breath and heartbeat as he cradled her. To remind himself she was okay.

Once they made it to her place, he reset the alarm to stay mode and stripped out of his suit. Leaving his boxers on, he fell onto her bed without bothering to pull the comforter back. She didn't bother either. She shimmied out of her formfitting dress to reveal she hadn't been wearing a bra, but she didn't take her panties off before curling up next to him. In the morning he knew exactly how he'd be waking her up. He smiled at the thought and closed his eyes.

She threw her leg over him and sighed contentedly as she settled her head against his chest. The way she snuggled up so tight in his embrace made his chest tighten. Especially after what had happened only hours ago. He'd seen too many friends die when he'd been stationed overseas, but almost losing Eve would have been too much to bear.

The realization that he couldn't walk away from her hit him with the intensity of a semi-truck. He wanted her in his bed and his life all the time. If anything had happened to Eve, he'd never have forgiven himself for not protecting her. And the thought of living without her? He shuddered, not able to even think it.

She'd always been in his life and in his thoughts. Even when he'd been overseas, her face had often been the one he dreamed of before drifting off to sleep. *She was alive*, he reminded himself for the hundredth time that night. Tightening his hold, he let the blackness of sleep overtake him.

* * *

Mac's eyes flew open to a quiet darkness. His heart pounded loud in his ears as he slowly sat up, every sense on alert. Something was different.

It took a moment to realize that the numbers of the digital clock on Eve's nightstand no longer illuminated the room in a dull, green glow. And the low hum from her refrigerator he'd all but tuned out was now silent.

Slowly, he reached for where he'd set his gun on the nightstand and slipped out of bed. No one was going to hurt Eve.

She murmured something, but otherwise didn't stir. He crept toward her window and slowly pulled the gold curtain back a fraction.

The back porch light of her neighbor's house was on. Which meant only her power had shut off. Or more likely it had been turned off by someone. He pulled the curtain back farther to give himself a little more light.

Silently he hurried back to Eve's sleeping form. He rustled her awake and put his free hand over her mouth when she started to speak.

He leaned forward so that his mouth was practically on her ear. "Someone's here. Call the cops and stay in the closet until I come get you. Tell them to leave their sirens off." His clipped instructions were lower than a whisper, but she heard him.

With wide eyes she nodded and sat up. Before she headed to the closet, she pulled out a small case from under her bed and withdrew a gun of her own. Then she plucked her cell phone from her nightstand.

He breathed easier as he watched her move to the relative safety of her closet. Once the door slid closed behind her, he eased open her bedroom door. The hallway was dark, only illuminated by slim streams of moonlight coming in from the guest bedroom door that was ajar. When he heard slight movement from somewhere else in the house, he paused.

It sounded like it came from the living room. His feet were silent as he stole down the hallway. Once he reached the end of it, he pressed his back against the wall and listened again.

An almost imperceptible squeak pulsed through the air. Eve's living room was carpeted but the attached hallway was plank wood floors. That hallway connected with the one Mac was now in.

Instead of moving against the intruder—or intruders—he stayed where he was and waited. Whoever was here expected the element of surprise.

They would have had it too if they hadn't turned off the power. The sudden quiet had been damn near deafening to him. Of course if they hadn't turned it off, they wouldn't have gotten past Eve's security system.

They weren't getting past him.

A scant shadow stretched across the floor in front of Mac. As it grew wider, Mac tensed, ready to fight more than one assailant if necessary. If Eve had already placed the call he hoped it wouldn't be long until the cops got here.

But he wasn't counting on them. He was the only defense between Eve and whoever was in her house. And he'd be damned if he let anyone hurt her.

There was another soft squeak and Mac crouched slightly. He clutched the gun in one hand and when the shadow grew wider he knew the intruder was close. The faint breathing of someone grew louder and louder so he made his move.

Gun in hand, Mac kept his stance low as he jumped out from his hiding position.

A dark-haired man wearing all black jerked back in surprise but started to raise a gun. Mac lashed out with his foot, kicking the intruder's arm and taking him off guard. If he didn't have to kill him, he didn't want to.

122 | KATIE REUS

If there was more than one person after Eve, Mac wanted to know their names. She couldn't live in a state of constant fear of being targeted. And he wouldn't allow it.

The man cried out as his gun flew through the air. It clattered against the wall but instead of retreating, the intruder lunged at Mac. With his free hand, Mac hauled back and slammed his fist against the other man's jaw. He knew how to fight and shoot with both hands and relished the feel of his fist connecting with this bastard.

Another cry rang out as the man flew back and this time he slammed against the wall. When he made a move to dive for his fallen weapon, Mac fired off a shot near the gun. Immediately the man held up his hands in surrender. He cursed under his breath before he said, "Don't shoot."

"Face down on the floor and keep your hands behind your head." There was a deadly edge to his voice that left no doubt he'd kill the man if necessary. After the man did as Mac ordered, he used his foot to kick the gun back behind himself. "Why are you after Eve?"

When the man didn't answer, Mac kicked him in the ribs. He'd never been one to abuse a prisoner but this guy had come after Eve with the intent to kill her. Maybe worse. There weren't many reasons someone broke into a woman's house in the middle of the night armed with a gun. This guy was lucky he was still breathing.

"She was a loose end," he grunted.

A loose end? Mac growled softly under his breath. As flashing red and blue lights filtered through the slats of the blinds in the living room, they lit up the hallway. Even though blood rushed in his ears from the rage building inside him, his breathing evened out as it sank in that this was hopefully almost over. Once the police got this guy into custody, it would only be a matter of time before Tara and this intruder fought over who could make the better deal.

"Eve? You can come out now! It's safe." And he planned to make sure she stayed that way.

CHAPTER THIRTEEN

One Week Later

Eve looked at her packed suitcase and fought the sadness welling up inside her. She should be happy. Tara and a man named Oscar Perez were both going to jail on so many charges it made her head spin. They'd both tried to make deals but with murder, kidnapping, breaking and entering, distribution of narcotics and a whole mess of other stuff they were being charged with, neither one of them was walking away without doing some serious time. Tara had given up the location of Martin's body, which she'd left abandoned in the desert in the back of her father's 'stolen' car.

It also looked like the cops would be making more arrests they hadn't planned on. Oscar agreed to testify against some of his thugs in exchange for a shorter sentence. Eve didn't think he'd last very long in prison once word got out he'd flipped on his own guys but that was his problem.

Now that she was safe, she could move home. She and Mac had spent every night together at his place since the cops had arrested Oscar Perez breaking into her home, but after a week she knew she couldn't stay here indefinitely.

Mac hadn't said anything about a future and even though she knew this wasn't casual, she couldn't very well move in with him. It was way too soon. Not for her, but he'd been a bachelor for a long time. If they moved too fast she'd probably scare him off and that was the last thing she wanted.

She rolled her suitcase into the foyer and left it there before heading to the living room. It was Friday night, which meant Mac's cook wasn't coming in. The guys who were off for the night would likely head into town to one of the local bars. Mac hadn't said it, but she guessed he probably wanted some guy time. They'd practically lived and breathed each other for the last week and she didn't want to smother him. Even if her heart ached at the thought of leaving, she didn't want to screw up the best thing that had ever happened to her by forcing her way into all aspects of his life.

While she waited, she flipped on his giant, flat screen television. She shook her head as the surround sound came on, nearly deafening her. He might be a roughneck rancher but the man sure liked his toys.

As she turned the volume down she heard the door to his kitchen opening. Fighting the dread that burned through her, she pressed the mute button and went to meet him.

Wearing a long-sleeved flannel shirt, dirty jeans and dusty boots, he looked good enough to eat. His face broke into a smile when he saw her. "Hey, darlin'." He dropped a brief but searing kiss on her mouth before grabbing a beer from the fridge. As he popped the top, he frowned at her. He looked her over from head to toe and suddenly looked nervous. "Did we make plans to go out tonight?"

Smiling, she shook her head. She wore a formfitting V-neck sweater and tight jeans that showed off all her assets because if she was headed home tonight, she wanted to leave him with a nice picture of her. "No. I figured it was time to give you your house back. I appreciate you letting me stay here all week. The thought of sleeping in my house after that man was in there creeped me out, but knowing he's going to jail makes me feel better. I cleaned up your bathroom and I think I got all my clothes but if I forgot something I can grab it later." She snapped her mouth shut when she realized she was rambling.

Nervously, she cleared her throat. He stared at her with those icy blue eyes, not saying a word. She'd thought he'd be relieved to have his space back, but he looked almost angry. Finally he spoke. "Have I made you feel unwelcome here?"

"No."

He set his beer on the counter next to him and took a step toward her, his expression growing darker. "Do you want to go home?"

She shrugged. Of course she didn't want to. "I'm sure you want your place back to yourself."

"That's not an answer." His words were a soft growl that sent a shiver down her spine.

"I...what do you want me to say? I didn't think you'd appreciate me shacking up at your place indefinitely. I thought I'd save you the trouble of having to awkwardly ask me to leave." She figured he'd be relieved she'd taken this step but his face said otherwise.

He stepped closer until they were a foot apart, his blue eyes blazing. His spicy, earthy scent surrounded her. "So you're walking away from us?"

"No. I'm going home." She crossed her arms over her chest defensively.

He made a strangled, annoyed sound. Then he cursed, loudly and abrasively. She stared at him as he let loose a string of words she'd never heard him utter before.

"*Stay*, Eve."

She bit her bottom lip, unsure exactly what he meant. "I'm not leaving for good or anything. I still want to date you and—"

"Fuck that. I want more than dating. Move in with me."

Her eyes widened in shock. "What?"

He pushed out a long, frustrated sigh. "I thought you understood how I feel about you. I don't want to do the back and forth thing with you, especially when I know you're *it* for me. I don't want to just date because I don't want to see anyone else. I want to see you every morning when I wake up and every night when I come home. I don't live that much farther from town than you do. You can keep your house if you want. Hell, I'll pay the mortgage on it. Just don't leave."

At his declaration, all the air sucked from her lungs in a whoosh. Mac had never been particularly vocal about anything. Of course she hadn't said anything about the future either so maybe she was to blame too for assuming he'd want his house back to himself.

For a moment she wondered if it would be a mistake, but she knew what she craved from him. She'd wanted the man since she was too young to even know *what* she wanted. Her attraction and love for him hadn't waned in over a decade. A slow smile broke out over her face. "I have a lot of clothes and shoes. You'll have to make room in your closet if you're serious."

At her words his face relaxed. He grabbed her hips possessively, pulling her tight against him. Through their clothes, his erection was hard and insistent. "I'll give you the whole damn thing if you'll move in here. I love you, Eve. Have for a long time. This past week I've been working up to telling you and hoping you didn't throw me out on my ass."

She snorted softly. "I love you too, Mac."

She'd barely gotten the words out before his mouth crushed over hers. His fingers clamped tighter around her hips and he lifted her until she wrapped her legs around his waist. As their lips and tongues danced in a hungry erotic rhythm, she felt him walking them back to his room.

No doubt they were in for a long night. And she couldn't wait.

Thank you for reading Killer Secrets. I really hope you enjoyed it and that you'll consider leaving a review at one of your favorite online retailers. It's a great way to help other readers discover new books. I appreciate all reviews.

If you liked Killer Secrets and would like to read more, turn the page for a sneak peek of Bound to Danger, the second book in my Deadly Ops series. And if you don't want to miss any future releases, please feel free to join my newsletter. I only send out a newsletter for new releases or sales news. Find the signup link on my website: http://www.katiereus.com

BOUND TO DANGER

Deadly Ops Series
Copyright © 2014 Katie Reus

Forcing her body to obey her when all she wanted to do was curl into a ball and cry until she passed out, she got up. Cool air rushed over her exposed back and backside as her feet hit the chilly linoleum floor. She wasn't wearing any panties and the hospital gown wasn't covering much of her. She didn't care.

Right now she didn't care about much at all.

Sometime when she'd been asleep her dirty, rumpled gown had been removed from the room. And someone had left a small bag of clothes on the bench by the window. No doubt Nash had brought her something to wear. He'd been in to see her a few times, but she'd asked him to leave each time. She felt like a complete bitch because she knew he just wanted to help, but she didn't care. Nothing could help, and being alone with her pain was the only way she could cope right now.

Feeling as if she were a hundred years old, she'd started unzipping the small brown leather bag when the door opened. As she turned to look over her shoulder, she found Nash, a uniformed police officer, and another really tall, thuggish-looking man entering.

Her eyes widened in recognition. The tattoos were new, but the *thug* was Cade O'Reilly. He'd served in the Marines with her brother. They'd been best friends and her brother, Riel, named after her father, had even brought him home a few times. But that was years ago. Eight to be exact. It was hard to forget the man who'd completely cut her out of his life after her brother died, as if she meant nothing to him.

Cade towered over Nash—who was pretty tall himself—and had a sleeve of tattoos on one arm and a couple on the other. His jet-black hair was almost shaved, the skull trim close to his head, just like the last time she'd seen him. He was . . . intimidating. Always had been. And startlingly handsome in that bad-boy way she was sure had made plenty of women . . . Yeah, she wasn't even going there.

She swiveled quickly, putting her back to the window so she wasn't flashing them. Reaching around to her back, she clasped the hospital gown together. "You can't knock?" she practically shouted, her voice raspy from crying, not sure whom she was directing the question to.

"I told them you weren't to be bothered, but—"

The police officer cut Nash off, his gaze kind but direct. "Ms. Cervantes, this man is from the NSA and needs to ask you some questions. As soon as you're done, the doctors will release you."

"I know who he is." She bit the words out angrily, earning a surprised look from Nash and a controlled look from Cade.

She might know Cade, or she had at one time, but she hadn't known he worked for the NSA. After her brother's death he'd stopped communicating with her. Her brother had brought him home during one of their short leaves, and she and Cade had become friends. *Good friends.* They'd e-mailed all the time, for almost a year straight. Right near the end of their long correspondence, things had shifted between them, had been heading into more than friendly territory. Then after Riel died, it was as if Cade had too. It had cut her so deep to lose him on top of her brother. And now he showed up in the hospital room after her mom's death and wanted to talk to her? Hell no.

She'd been harassing the nurses to find a doctor who would discharge her, and now she knew why they'd been putting her off. They'd done a dozen tests and she didn't have a brain injury. She wasn't exhibiting any signs of having a concussion except for the memory loss, but the doctors were convinced that this was because of shock and trauma at what she'd apparently witnessed.

Nash started to argue, but the cop hauled him away, talking in low undertones, shutting the door behind them. Leaving her alone with this giant of a man.

Feeling raw and vulnerable, Maria wrapped her arms around herself. The sun had almost set, so even standing by the window didn't warm her up. She just felt so damn cold. Because of the room and probably grief. And now to be faced with a dark reminder of her past was too much.

COMPLETE BOOKLIST

Red Stone Security Series
No One to Trust
Danger Next Door
Fatal Deception
Miami, Mistletoe & Murder
His to Protect
Breaking Her Rules
Protecting His Witness
Sinful Seduction
Under His Protection

The Serafina: Sin City Series
First Surrender
Sensual Surrender
Sweetest Surrender

Deadly Ops Series
Targeted
Bound to Danger

Non-series Romantic Suspense
Running From the Past
Everything to Lose
Dangerous Deception

Dangerous Secrets
Killer Secrets
Deadly Obsession
Danger in Paradise
His Secret Past

Paranormal Romance
Destined Mate
Protector's Mate
A Jaguar's Kiss
Tempting the Jaguar
Enemy Mine
Heart of the Jaguar

Moon Shifter Series
Alpha Instinct
Lover's Instinct (novella)
Primal Possession
Mating Instinct
His Untamed Desire (novella)
Avenger's Heat
Hunter Reborn

Darkness Series
Darkness Awakened
Taste of Darkness

ABOUT THE AUTHOR

Katie Reus is the *New York Times* and *USA Today* bestselling author of the Red Stone Security series, the Moon Shifter series and the Deadly Ops series. She fell in love with romance at a young age thanks to books she pilfered from her mom's stash. Years later she loves reading romance almost as much as she loves writing it.

However, she didn't always know she wanted to be a writer. After changing majors many times, she finally graduated summa cum laude with a degree in psychology. Not long after that she discovered a new love. Writing. She now spends her days writing dark paranormal romance and sexy romantic suspense.

For more information on Katie please visit her website: www.katiereus.com. Also find her on twitter @katiereus or visit her on facebook at: www.facebook.com/katiereusauthor.

67222204R00086

Made in the USA
Lexington, KY
05 September 2017